# THE TALK OF THE TOWN

DAUGHTERS OF THE
GREAT DEPRESSION

# THE TALK OF THE TOWN

## FRAN BAKER

**FIVE STAR**
*A part of Gale, Cengage Learning*

GALE
CENGAGE Learning·

Detroit • New York • San Francisco • New Haven, Conn • Waterville, Maine • London

# GALE
CENGAGE Learning™

**LIBRARY OF CONGRESS CATALOGING-IN-PUBLICATION DATA**

Baker, Fran, 1947–.
   The talk of the town : daughters of the Great Depression / Fran Baker. — 1st ed.
    p. cm.
   ISBN-13: 978-1-4328-2539-3 (hardcover)
   ISBN-10: 1-4328-2539-9 (hardcover)
   1. Ex-convicts—Fiction. I. Title.
PS3552.A4265T36 2011
813'.54—dc22                          2011021802

First Edition. First Printing: September 2011.
Published in 2011 in conjunction with Tekno Books.

In Loving Memory Of
Ruth Catherine McKenzie McCoy
I still miss you, Mom

# CHAPTER 1

*Blue Ridge, Missouri; 1933*

Agnes Dill started it. After hoovering up a generous slice of buttermilk pie along with a brimming handful of mixed nuts, the plump widow declared in no uncertain terms that she would be double-checking her door locks from now on. In what had to be a first, everyone in the overheated parlor nodded their heads in agreement.

Everyone, that is, but Roxie Mitchell.

Roxie's ink pen fell still and her secretary's journal almost slid off her lap as she stared at the other women in genuine astonishment. Accord wasn't common among the members of the Ladies Aide. Far from it, actually. Whether discussing something as important as the monthly bake sales that raised money for charities like the town library and the orphan's home, or even something as mundane as what china piece would be handed out at the Pharaoh Theatre's next Dish Night, the women could usually be counted on for an hour or two of debate.

Not today, however. Even Violet Lynch had agreed with Agnes. And this after last month's meeting when Violet had insisted that Agnes didn't have enough brains to fill a dressmaker's thimble.

A mischievous impulse, or perhaps that streak of rebelliousness that her mother had so often complained about, compelled Roxie to dissent.

"Isn't that a tad dramatic?" she asked in a voice tinged with amusement.

No sooner did the words leave her mouth than nine china cups clattered into their matching saucers, nine heads swiveled in her direction, and nine pairs of eyes focused sharply on her.

Ignoring the fact that she was now the center of attention, she capped her pen, closed her journal, then picked up her cup and took a sip of tea that had grown distastefully tepid in the time since it had been served. The pendulum clock on the wall of the stuffy room ticked loudly in the silence and the unseasonably cold late April wind had the tree branches tap-tap-tapping at the panes of the brocade-draped windows. In the corner stove a hearty fire snapped, crackled and popped.

Roxie heard each sound distinctly as she waited for a response to her question.

It wasn't long in coming. Mabel Foltzcroft, wife of the town's physician and hostess for this afternoon's meeting, was the first to recover. Like a marionette whose strings had been yanked, she sat erect in her horsehair chair and posed a question of her own.

"Dramatic?" Mabel's red Tangee lipstick bled into the lines around her puckered-up mouth. "What do you mean, dramatic?"

Roxie took the time to set her tea cup in its matching saucer on the small table beside her chair and to smile around the room before replying. No one smiled back. Regardless, she willed herself to finish what she had started.

"It's just that everyone seems to be making such a big fuss about him. After all, it's not as if he's"—she searched for an innocuous comparison to make her point and the best she could come up with was—"some crazed debaucher turned loose on the town."

"We all know *precisely* what he is," Mabel said in a tone that was just this side of snide.

The other women bobbed their heads in support of that pronouncement.

"Then you also know what he isn't." Roxie's vehemence surprised her as much as it apparently did the others. Her earlier amusement had completely subsided, deflated by a prick of annoyance. What was the matter with all of them, anyway? Weren't they even going to give him a chance? "He's not Public Enemy Number One."

Knowing looks passed from one woman to another, arcing around the circle in a matter of seconds. It wasn't the first time Roxie had taken up for the underdog. She'd made a habit of it her whole life, so no one could really claim to be surprised that she was doing so now. This time, though, their looks seemed to say, she'd gone too far.

"It never hurts to take precautions." Roxie's sister-in-law Marlene hadn't quite recovered her figure after giving birth to her third son almost six months ago, but that hadn't kept her from giving Agnes some stiff competition in the refreshments-gobbling department. Nor did the fact that she was married to Roxie's oldest brother and supposedly bound by at least a semblance of family loyalty forestall a public chastising. "You'll realize that once you have children."

"She'd best get married first," put in the newly-wed Rose Dirks.

Polite coughs and a subtle clearing of throats muffled the ensuing titters.

Roxie knew what prompted their reaction. It was the very same thing they gossiped about over their back fences or whispered to each other when she left a room. Roxie Mitchell was too opinionated, too educated, too much her own woman. And at twenty-five her chances of finding a suitable man to marry were growing slimmer by the day.

As the room grew quiet again, her reproving blue gaze swept the circle. She knew she should let the matter drop and end the meeting on a note of camaraderie. But the bur was under her skin now and wouldn't let her be.

"Even if I had a dozen children, it wouldn't change my opinion," she said. "I think you're all overreacting. He's back barely one day, and you're ready to run him out of town on a rail."

"Well, what would you have us do?" Candise Sherman glanced up from the toe of the black sock she was darning for her corset salesman husband. "Welcome him back with a party?"

"Fete him like the Prodigal Son?" demanded the preacher's wife, Margaret Pierce, in a voice that was rife with righteous indignation.

"That wild Bauer boy will probably have his own party," Agnes Dill—the woman who had started it all—asserted with a decided sniff that said what kind of party she thought it would be.

"He's not a boy anymore," Roxie reminded her when she could get a word in edgewise.

"Which makes him more dangerous than ever," Agnes replied on a bite.

Tongues clicked in concurrence. Roxie had to stifle hers to keep from shouting at her lifelong friends. At the same time, she wondered why she felt so strongly. What, after all, did it matter to her? She didn't care anything about Luke Bauer. She'd hardly known him and that mostly by reputation. Yet she not only continued to defend him but she also gave them something else to chew on.

"Well, he didn't look very dangerous to me," she said in a deliberately provocative tone.

Once again, all eyes riveted on Roxie.

"You *saw* him?" Candise squealed.

"When?" Mabel asked.

"On my way here."

"Where?"

"He was walking away from the train station when I dropped my car off at Hubbard's Garage." Roxie drove a 1923 Model T, and this was the third time in the six months since she'd bought it that the ten-year-old car had been in for service. Still, she couldn't complain too awfully much because she'd only paid twenty-five dollars for it when Terrence and Sandra Riley sold out and moved in with their Kansas City relatives. "He didn't look any different from anyone else, just a regular person."

That wasn't precisely true, she acknowledged to herself. He hadn't looked like a regular person at all. On the contrary, from the moment he'd stepped off the arrival platform, and started down the sidewalk, he'd stood out from everyone else. Perhaps it was the unruly black hair that the wind tossed every which way. Or the ill-fitting suit he'd clearly outgrown while in prison. It might even have been the battered brown suitcase in which he appeared to carry all his worldly possessions. Regardless, he was all dark good looks and attitude—exactly the type of man a woman couldn't take her eyes off of and other men crossed the street to avoid.

And avoid him was exactly what they'd done.

Roxie had paused after coming out of the garage and watched in appalled fascination as the women who'd seen him walking their way had goggled and blushed before stepping into the doorway of the nearest store. The men were no less obvious. Those who hadn't blatantly crossed the street had given him wide berth on the sidewalk. She'd been ashamed of them, all of them, in that moment.

But was she any better? She chastised herself now. Did she really have any room to judge their actions? Not knowing what else to do, she had just turned on her heel and practically run the three blocks to Mabel's house.

Now Mabel gave her freshly waved and hennaed hair a self-important pat. "Luke Bauer never looked like anybody else."

"Didn't act like anybody else, either," Margaret added on a disdainful note. "Seemed to think he could live by his own rules."

Julia Murphy, the town librarian and today's speaker, looked up from the pillowcase she had recommenced embroidering after refreshments. "He always was a loner."

Rose shivered. "Had a way of looking right through a body that turned my blood to ice."

"Pride." Candise moved her wooden darning egg to the heel of her husband's sock and squinted at the small hole she found there. "That was his problem."

"*One* of his problems," Mabel qualified.

Busy sorting cotton squares for the postage stamp quilt she planned to make, Virginia Jones had remained silent throughout this uncharitable exchange. Now she looked up from the small pile of colorful squares.

"As I recall, he was always polite as a boy, always minded his manners whenever he brought honey or fruit from his grand-father's farm into the store to sell," she said, speaking on Luke Bauer's behalf. Virginia and her husband owned the Blue Ridge General Store, where most of the Ladies Aide members did their weekly shopping. "He never took a piece of candy from me or from David without saying thank you. There was good in him back then. Perhaps there still is."

"Oh, Virginia, you'd make excuses for the devil himself, you would," Mabel said with a dismissive wave of her hand.

Once again everyone nodded in agreement.

And once again, Roxie was the odd woman out. "But maybe Virginia's right," she argued with renewed vigor. "Maybe there's good in him yet."

Disbelief sharpened Mabel's expression.

Roxie glanced at Virginia, who nodded encouragingly, and then said in a rush, "We should at least give him a chance to earn our respect and our trust."

"There's such a thing as being too trusting." Violet's voice held almost as much sorrow as her eyes when she lifted them from the gray silk dress she'd been hemming and met Roxie's gaze.

An uncomfortable silence descended over the sitting room as talk of Luke Bauer ceased and they all tried vainly not to remember how Paul Lynch had deserted Violet, just up and walked out on her and their two daughters last year, leaving Violet to eke out a meager living for herself and her children from her alterations business.

"You'll learn someday that it really doesn't pay to trust too much." The quavery way Violet said it added impact to her words.

Feeling her throat tighten with that familiar ache, the unbearable pain and secret shame that had driven her back home, Roxie swallowed hard. Violet was right. There *was* such a thing as being too trusting. She had learned that lesson the hard way. Arthur had taught it to her with humiliating thoroughness.

"That's true, Violet, sadly true," Mabel said in a patronizing tone before bouncing back to her original point. Focusing on Roxie now, she reiterated, "And you certainly can't trust a Bauer. It's in the blood."

Her comment sparked others just as cutting.

"Bad blood, those Bauers."

"I can't ever remember seeing Everett Bauer draw a sober breath."

"Or do a day's honest work."

"Wound up in a pauper's grave, you know."

"And what about that Nadene?"

"She came from a good family," someone said in her defense.

"Well, a fine mother she turned out to be, running off with that traveling salesman when her boy was still in nappies," someone else rejoined.

"Would you have stayed with Everett? He was a drunkard with a bad temper."

"Maybe not, but I wouldn't have left my baby behind."

Roxie let the gossip swirl around her, wishing she'd never started this conversation. She didn't know why she'd felt so compelled to argue on Luke Bauer's behalf, anyway. If she'd ever said more than a couple words to him in her life, she couldn't recall it. In fact, she really couldn't remember much about him, period. It had all been so many years ago . . .

She stared down at her lap, not seeing the journal in which she'd scribbled her notes about the upcoming library fundraiser but instead envisioning the darkly handsome youth with the defiant look and daredevil laugh who'd never really fit in with the rest of the kids in town. Yes, he'd been proud and wild and a loner. Always the troublemaker. Always the rabble rouser looking for a good fight. Always the town's bad boy.

But the town's bad boy was all grown up now. He didn't need Roxie Mitchell—or anyone else, for that matter—sticking up for him. He could fight his own battles.

And what, she wondered idly, would the man be like?

That thought brought her up short. Roxie blinked and raised her head. The muted glow of lamplight cast shadowed crescents throughout the room, highlighting some of the women's features and shading others. Every face she saw was as familiar to her as her own reflection in the mirror each morning. She'd known all of them all her life. And in a small town like this, that meant she knew their likes and dislikes. She knew without asking that Mabel took sugar in her tea but not in her coffee, that Marlene took sugar in, and on, everything she put in her mouth, and that Julia never took sugar at all. She knew that they all did their washing on Mondays, their ironing on Tuesdays and the bulk of their shopping on Saturdays.

And she knew that each of them knew almost as much about her. It wasn't nosiness so much as it was life in a small town where everybody knew everybody else and their business. But it was that very lack of privacy coupled with the desire to go places, to see and do things she couldn't see or do here that had prompted her to strike out on her own when she graduated from Blue Ridge High School.

As the youngest and only girl in a family of four children, she had often craved the luxury of being left alone to read or think or dream. That was more of a rarity than reality, though. Before Wall Street went bust in 1929 and took most of the nation's financial institutions with it, her banker father and busy housewife mother had maintained an open door policy when it came to family, neighbors and friends. Add in frequent overnight visits from her grandparents, aunts and uncles and cousins, and her childhood home had been filled to the rafters with noise and laughter and, at times, utter confusion.

And then there were her parents' expectations. It went without saying that Roxie's brothers would go to college. After all, a man needed a profession in order to properly support his family. But Roxie . . . well, it was pretty much a given that she would marry a fine, upstanding townsman and produce a passel of grandchildren for her parents to pamper and spoil.

But their hopes for her were dashed when, early in her senior year of high school, Roxie announced that her business teacher had praised her aptitude for the subject and had encouraged her to further her studies at Stephens Women's College in Columbia, Missouri. Her mother had pooh-poohed the idea, not wanting her only daughter to go so far away, and her father had refused to even consider it, claiming that a woman didn't need a college education to raise a family.

Their opposition not only hadn't deterred her, but it had had the opposite effect. Rather than pout or cry or throw a tantrum, she had pondered the problem for several days before she finally decided how best to solve it. Once she had figured out what to say, she made an appointment to meet her father in his office at the bank. There, she had made a very deliberate case for continuing her education. First, she had reminded him that she had inherited his head for numbers and that it would be a terrible shame to let that gift go to waste. Then she had urged him to consider how she would support herself in the unlikely instance she never married. Finally she took the practical approach, pretty much catching him off-guard when she asked him for a bank loan to meet her college expenses and promised to pay it back with interest.

Her arguments had won her the day. Over her mother's ongoing objections, he put up the money out of his own pocket to enroll her at Stephens. His only condition was that she finished what she started.

She did, graduating with a degree in business and highest honors. Then she'd taken another step toward declaring her independence. She'd settled in St. Louis, where she'd rented a room in a nice, clean boardinghouse and had gone to work as a bookkeeper for a dress manufacturing company.

At first she loved it. She loved the noise and the culture and the constant traffic. She loved shouldering her way through a crowd of strangers, none of them knowing who she was, where she was going or why. She loved eating new and, to her, exotic foods like Italian sausage and German sauerkraut. She loved watching the boats and barges ply the Mississippi River, attending lectures at the Botanical Garden or taking leisurely strolls around Forest Park after church on Sundays. Most of all, she loved not having to share her every waking moment with someone else.

But in the end, Roxie had come back to Blue Ridge a sadder yet wiser woman. And now Luke Bauer had come back, too. With even less reason to—she, after all, had returned to the loving comfort of family and friends—he'd come back to Blue Ridge.

It seemed to Roxie that she was on the verge of making some significant correlation about all this when Mabel interrupted her thoughts by announcing that the meeting was adjourned. Only then did she realize that everyone else was standing, smoothing out their skirts and making one last comment or suggestion about which books to buy with the proceeds from the library fundraiser. She smiled contritely as she put her notebook and pen in her clutch purse and stood.

"I'm sorry," she said to no one in particular as she followed the others to the entry hall to retrieve her coat and hat.

"Woolgathering, Roxie?" Julia asked.

Preoccupied with tilting her tweed beret at a jaunty angle and belting the brown wool jersey jacket that had served her so well for four years running, Roxie let the question pass without an answer.

"She must have been thinking about some man," Candise teased as she tucked her husband's newly darned socks into her handbag. "Only a man can make a woman that dreamy in the middle of one of *our* meetings."

The women's laughter followed them out of the overheated house and into the chilly afternoon, where everyone continued visiting before saying their final goodbyes and going their separate ways.

That rebelliousness of Roxie's rose up again. As a gust of wind blew across the white-painted front porch, she smiled at Candise and said, "As a matter of fact, I was."

Candise looked at her in confusion. "Was what?"

"Thinking about a man." Roxie let her words hang in the snappy air for a few seconds before clarifying. "I was thinking about Luke Bauer."

The women's laughing and talking stopped abruptly. An engine backfire that sounded like a rifle shot filled the sudden silence as the coal man's old B-model pickup rumbled down the street. The afternoon school bell, which could be heard ringing from one end of town to the other, signaled to mothers that their children would soon be home and hungry for cookies and milk.

Despite the chill wind, Mabel held the door open and poked her head out so as not to miss anything being said by the other women.

"Now, Roxie—" Julia began.

"What do you mean, you were thinking about Luke Bauer?" Marlene's lips pursed up as tight as her corset laces as she peered fixedly at her sister-in-law from beneath the brim of her plate-shaped hat.

"I was just wondering how he'll adjust is all," Roxie answered with a nonchalant shrug.

A chorus of harrumphs said the other women didn't share her concern.

"What's going on here, Roxie?" Marlene demanded.

She knew what Marlene meant but wasn't about to give her the satisfaction of saying so. "Nothing."

"Was there"—now Marlene hesitated briefly—"something between you two all those years ago?"

The sheer inanity of the question startled Roxie out of her bedeviling mood. She gaped at Marlene in amazement for a full minute, keenly aware that everyone's eyes were upon her, before she finally spoke. "Who? Me?"

Marlene continued to regard her sternly. "Yes, Roxie, you. You and Luke Bauer."

"Of course not!" Roxie cried. "How could you think such a thing? We didn't even know each other."

"He was in the same class as your brother John," Marlene reminded her.

"But I was more interested in books than in boys." Roxie wished she didn't sound quite so defensive but knew she had no one to blame but herself for her present predicament. "Honestly, Marlene, Luke Bauer probably wouldn't know me from—from the tobacco store Indian."

Intent lines puckered around her sister-in-law's eyes. "Then why are you so concerned about him?"

"I'm not. I was just . . ." At a loss, Roxie let her voice trail off. She couldn't really deny that she felt concern, because she did. But not because she had any feelings for Luke Bauer—at least not the kind that Marlene was implying at any rate. In hopes of clearing the air, she blurted out, "I was just trying to say that I'd like to see people give him the benefit of the doubt, and I obviously didn't express it well. That's it. Nothing more, nothing less."

The other women remained silent, but Roxie could see that Marlene wasn't buying her explanation.

"I admire your sense of justice," Marlene said, though the annoyed set of her mouth declared the exact opposite. "But you don't want to get mixed up with him. A nice woman like you doesn't want to waste her time or risk her reputation with a convict."

"*Ex*-convict," Roxie corrected before she could stop herself.

Worry flashed over Marlene's round face. She glanced at the circle of women who were avidly listening to this exchange before returning her uneasy gaze to Roxie. "Maybe I should discuss this with Father and Mother Mitchell."

"Don't be ridiculous, Marlene." It was bad enough that her brother Bill would be hearing all the juicy details from his wife.

19

The last thing Roxie wanted was to cause her parents any more worry than she already had. "I'm not mixed up with Luke Bauer. Nor am I about to get mixed up with him. Believe me, if I did, you'd know about it. *Everybody* would know about it."

Marlene wavered. "You're sure?"

"Of course I'm sure. Around here, you can't sneeze without everyone saying 'God bless you.' "

Scandalized gasps punctuated her pronouncement.

Roxie offered a placating smile to one and all, noticing as she did that the wind was playing havoc with Mabel's recently-dressed hair. "I'm sorry. But I can't help making fun of such a ludicrous situation. I don't even know Luke Bauer, except for what's said about him, and I don't think I'll ever get to know him. So there's absolutely nothing for you or for anyone else to worry about. Okay?"

The other women, seeming to sense that things had been set right, began dispersing in various directions. A couple left in cars. Most, like Marlene, lived close enough to walk.

Now Marlene stepped off the porch but hovered uncertainly on the neatly swept front sidewalk. She looked down the street, toward her house, as if trying to calculate how much time she had before her two oldest boys got home from school. Her harried expression said that she thought she was cutting it close.

"Okay," she reluctantly agreed before shaking a chastising finger at Roxie. "But don't waste any more of your time or your sympathy on him. A man like that makes his own trouble, and there's no sense feeling sorry for him. Understood?"

"Understood." Roxie breathed a sigh of relief when Marlene turned away.

She made a point of waving goodbye to a wind-tousled Mabel, who finally closed her front door. Then she hurried down the porch steps and watched her sister-in-law turn for home. She had no doubt that she would be the main topic of conversation between Marlene and Bill tonight. Or that her entire family would soon be hearing about what happened at the meeting today.

So be it, Roxie thought as she tucked her purse under her arm, turned in the opposite direction from Marlene and started back toward Hubbard's Garage. She hadn't done anything wrong. Besides, she was a grown woman. She didn't have to answer to anyone—her sister-in-law included.

Still, she walked at a faster clip than usual, trying to outpace the sudden restlessness that had settled under her skin. Though it was cold and cloudy, she blamed her agitation on spring fever: on the new grass sprouting in patches of bright green, the daffodils tossing their lemony heads in the breeze, and the red-breasted robins busily building their nests in the branches of the budding trees.

But as she neared the corner, Roxie couldn't help feeling that it was fate rather than the wind at her back that was propelling her forward.

# CHAPTER 2

Roxie saw that he didn't recognize her and wondered at the tiny stab of—what? Disappointment? She knew that was absurd. As she'd insisted so stoutly a little over two weeks ago, she'd hardly even known him. She couldn't seriously expect him to remember her. Would she have remembered him if he'd been just another one of her brother John's schoolmates instead of "that wild Bauer boy" no one could forget?

They certainly hadn't forgotten. Town talk had been ample proof of that. Each disparaging remark had stirred her ever-ready sympathy for the underdog and was, she supposed now, why she'd felt compelled to see him. Of course, this interview would be nothing more than an empty gesture. But when Lana had left her switchboard post and ducked into Roxie's office to announce in a dramatic stage whisper that he was out front wanting work, she simply hadn't been able to turn him away.

Roxie had risen from behind her desk to greet him. She had found that it went far to help ease the surprise or shyness that could sometimes strike men who weren't expecting to talk to a woman. But the man who stood in her doorway now gave no indication of discomfort. In fact, he gave no indication of anything at all.

Sighing inwardly, she motioned him toward the straight-backed chair beside her desk. He crossed to it, leaving the door open behind him. Running her hand over the creases in her blue cotton skirt, she took her own seat as he slid soundlessly into the chair. Even seated he seemed to dominate the cramped office, his broad-shouldered shadow almost totally enveloping her as it blocked the dim overhead light. The silence stretched out as she fussed needlessly with a small stack of orders that needed to be filled and billed, wishing she'd not put herself in this unpleasant position. Finally she set the papers next to her typewriter, folded her hands on the desktop and looked at him.

She'd thought he would appear humbled by his recent imprisonment. She'd thought wrong.

Staring into his steely gray eyes, Roxie rapidly readjusted her thinking. She'd felt sorry for him, sorry for the years he'd wasted, sorry for the continual censure he had to endure. She'd felt a wave of pity when he'd entered her office wearing the same too-small suit he'd worn the day of his arrival. But looking at his hard, handsome face with those errant strands of thick black hair that refused to stay slicked-back and that thin scar streaking across his left cheekbone, she realized her mistake. This man didn't need her pity. He didn't look as if he needed anything or anyone at all.

She glanced down at her hands. She should be inquiring about his background, but she knew his background—everybody did. She should be testing his attitude, but she knew his attitude—and it wasn't the attitude one usually looked for in an employee. No one else had thought him a suitable applicant. She'd heard of several shopkeepers and area farmers who'd refused to hire him for even a day's work—not so much because they didn't need the help as because they didn't trust him.

She shouldn't have agreed to interview him, she realized. It could only lead to trouble. But it was too late to worry about that now. She had agreed to it, and she needed to get on with it.

Toward that end, she started the process by introducing herself. "I'm Roxie Mitchell."

"Luke Bauer," he replied politely.

The formalities behind them, she asked, "What kind of work are you looking for, Mr. Bauer?"

"I'll do anything," he answered.

Roxie didn't know what to say to that. She lowered her eyes and then raised them again. His seemed to be focused on the wall behind her, yet she had the distinct, uncomfortable impression he was precisely aware of her least movement.

Tossing aside that nonsense, she cleared her throat and went on. "We're a small company, Mr.—"

"I made overalls in prison," he said at the same time.

She hesitated, trying to think of a tactful way to phrase it, and finally settled on simple honesty. "I'm afraid that isn't much of a qualification for work here because we don't manufacture anything."

"I also did maintenance and custodial chores before I joined the road gang," he supplied.

"I see," she responded inanely.

"I'm willing to learn whatever I need to," he said after a pause that grew more awkward by the second. "I've been told I'm a quick learner."

"You never seemed much interested in learning back in school." She spoke without thinking, remembering the Luke Bauer of a decade or more ago.

Flickers of surprise passed through his eyes, and she could see that he hadn't expected her to make a remark like that. But how could he have? She hadn't expected it herself.

"We went to school together," she explained hastily.

His blank look prompted her to elucidate.

"Well, not together exactly," she amended. "You were in my brother John's class. John Mitchell," she emphasized, hoping that his full name would ring a bell. "I was three years behind you. Too young for you to have paid any mind to, I'm sure."

Now he studied her with open curiosity. His gaze traveled

over her slowly, taking stock of each feature within her oval face. His own face remained blank, expressing none of the masculine appreciation she normally received, as he took note of her big blue eyes, her small, straight nose with its scattering of freckles, her full lips. She decided it was like trying to read that secret decoder ring one of her brothers sent away for years ago. A message was there, but she couldn't decipher it.

"You don't look much like John," he finally said.

His remark brought a bubble of laughter to her lips. "I certainly hope not."

He stared at her without so much as cracking a smile.

Flustered by his lack of emotion, she went on to say more than she intended, certainly more than she should have. "I don't look much like anyone else in my family, either. I've always been told that. They're all tall, even my mother, and they have brown eyes and hair, while I'm on the shorter side, with blue eyes, and my hair is—well, I don't know what you'd call it, more blond than . . ."

Suddenly aware that she was prattling, she stopped and just sat there like the proverbial bump on a log.

"Not blond," he corrected her. "Honey-colored."

Roxie tilted her head in confusion. "I beg your pardon?"

"Your hair. It's the color of the honey my grandfather used to gather from his bees."

Almost of its own volition, her hand crept up to touch the hair that fell in soft waves just past her jaw. Honey-colored, she mused as her fingers twirled within a few strands. What a strange thing for him to have said. She suddenly realized that he was watching her and, self-consciously, she dropped her hand.

A gleam lit his silvery eyes, unsettling her further. Now this was more like the Luke Bauer the Ladies Aide members were talking about at their last meeting. The wolfish comment, the suggestive look in his eyes . . .

She straightened and sought to regain control of the interview. "Now, about—"

"You had another brother, as I recall," he said then, his dark brows drawing together thoughtfully.

"Two more, actually." She ticked off their names. "William— he's the oldest and is named for our father, but he goes by Bill. Then Frederick, who's two years younger than Bill but doesn't like to be called Fred. And John, of course, who's the same age as you—two years younger than Frederick and three years older than me."

Whether he remembered them or not, he managed to look as if he was actually interested in them. "They're all still living in Blue Ridge?"

No longer resisting being sidetracked, she nodded. "Bill sells insurance, Frederick manages the lumber yard on the south side of town, and John is farming our grandparents' old place."

"And your parents?" he asked then.

Roxie smiled with a daughter's love. "They're well, thank you. Father has kept the bank running in spite of the stock market crash and the financial disasters it spurred. And when Mother isn't helping my brother Bill's wife with their three sons, she volunteers her time at the county orphan's home."

His voice softened now. "I remember one time she brought a batch of oatmeal cookies still warm from the oven to our grade school class. To this day I don't think I've ever had a cookie that good."

"She'd feed the world if she could."

"The way things are going, she might have to."

That was her cue to get back to business. "Obviously you realize that times are hard, that people everywhere are feeling the pinch." When he only looked at her mutely, she continued, "What I'm trying to say is, our orders have slowed and jobs are at a premium nowadays, so—"

He scraped back his chair and rose in one fluid movement. Roxie tilted her head back as far as her neck would allow and gaped up at him. She could see that his jaw was tightly clamped shut, the muscles quivering as he stared down at her.

"I'm not much for games, Miss Mitchell, so let's end the charade." Though he was visibly struggling to contain his anger, his voice held no hint of emotion. "You can thank me for stopping by and I can thank you for your time. Then you can go back to what you were doing before I interrupted you."

He reached the door in a single step.

Roxie catapulted from her chair. "Wait!"

To her surprise, he did.

She knew that she should let him go, knew it was best for both of them if she did, knew that she should feel relieved that he understood the situation. But she didn't feel relieved. She felt pain and anger and embarrassment. Most of all, she felt a renewal of unbearable pity that he would so readily accept, even expect, rejection. She stared at his back, where his wide shoulders strained the seams of his suit jacket, wanting to tell him how sorry she was she couldn't help him, wanting to apologize for the way the town was treating him, wanting to somehow ease his pain.

"All that's available is part-time work," she said impetuously. "Filling stock orders in the warehouse and loading or unloading trucks on the dock if one of the regulars doesn't show up."

He said nothing, but he didn't have to speak. His tense stance loudly declared his skepticism.

The room seemed to be shrinking in size. Roxie could feel the wooden file cabinet closing in on her from the left, while the cement block wall crowded her from behind. She couldn't possibly hire a man like Luke Bauer. What would people say? She'd be the talk of the town!

Determined not to let the possibility of becoming grist for

the gossip mill keep her from doing what she thought was right, she moistened her dry lips. "The pay won't be much. Fifty cents a day, with a raise to one dollar if orders pick up again or someone quits and you come on full time."

He turned with slow deliberation. "Are you offering me a job?"

His insolent stare issued the real challenge, daring her to say that he'd misunderstood her, that she was doing nothing of the sort. It was the kind of cocksure arrogance one expected from him, the kind of look and tone that inevitably set people's backs up. And it was the perfect excuse for her to say no.

But Roxie drew a deep breath and did what she'd somehow known all along she would do. "Yes," she told him. "Subject to Mr. Stewart's approval when he returns next week, I'm offering you a job."

His insolence vanished like morning fog under the sun, though his posture remained rigid. So quickly she thought she might have imagined it, a spark of emotion flared in his eyes and then died. The tension seemed to drain from him as it did, and when he finally spoke, he spoke quietly.

"You don't have to do this," he told her. "You don't have to hire me out of pity."

She flinched, started to deny it, but then met his perceptive gaze and said instead, "I happen to think you're capable of the work."

"I know I am," he replied with resolution. "And I intend to fully earn my pay wherever I work. But I don't want to be given misplaced charity."

Bauer pride collided with Mitchell obstinacy as they took each other's measure across her desk. His reluctance to accept the job only increased her determination that he should have it, even if it meant that she had to round him up and haul him in on the days he was scheduled to work. Purposefully, she tore her gaze away from his and started toward the door.

"If you'll follow me," she said in a matter-of-fact tone of voice, "I'll introduce you to the warehouse foreman, who will tell you how to check in each morning to see if he needs you."

Passing him, her shoulder lightly brushed his arm. Her hair seemed to crackle, her scalp to tingle. She stiffened and, mustering what dignity she could, she strode out. She wasn't all that certain that he would follow her. Within seconds she realized just how much she wanted him to follow. Her heart sank to new depths as she paused in the hall. Should she wait? Walk on? Go back and confront him?

He came out of her office looking cool and composed. "Show me the warehouse," he said.

They walked side by side down a long, poorly lit concrete corridor that seemed narrower than usual to Roxie. Each step resounded with a hollow thump that echoed the hammering of her heart. As much as she wanted to, she couldn't ignore the crazy rhythm of her careening pulse. She told herself it wasn't the taut caution of his catlike movements. She told herself it wasn't the aura of strength, even danger, that emanated from him. If she felt like an overwound clock, her heart ticking frantically and her nerves tightly coiled, she assured herself it had nothing whatsoever to do with the man beside her.

She cast him a sidelong look. He unexpectedly met her glance with one of his own. Both quickly looked away.

It must be guilt, she concluded, and promptly fell victim to self-recriminations. Sweet cracker sandwich, she'd hired him! How could she? Had she lost her mind? What would Mr. Stewart say to having an ex-convict working in his warehouse? Especially one who'd served time for armed robbery! Oh, why did the Stewarts have to be in St. Joseph to visit their daughter who was pregnant with their first grandchild this weekend? Why couldn't Luke Bauer have waited to seek employment until Mr.

Stewart got back?

Roxie pulled herself up short. There was nothing to be gained from such thoughts. She'd done what she believed was right. If Layton Stewart disagreed with her decision, he could rectify it when he returned.

Striving to regain her usual composure, she at least succeeded in maintaining the outward appearance of it as she began speaking in a breathy staccato. "Layton Stewart built Stewart's Warehouse almost seven years ago."

"Right after I went to prison," Luke interjected.

It amazed her that he spoke so candidly about being incarcerated. "Mr. Stewart likes to say we have harmony of place, and that's really not far from the truth. Being situated just a mile or so off Route 40 as well as on the rail line, Blue Ridge is perfectly located for what we do."

"Which is what, exactly?"

"We warehouse products—work boots, socks, shirts and what-have-you—for various manufacturers who don't have their own storage facilities, and then we distribute them throughout the Midwest."

"So you're kind of a middleman?"

His acumen impressed her. "And we ship by truck all over the state of Missouri and the western half of Kansas, and by rail beyond."

"Given the sorry state of the economy, I'm surprised to hear there's any kind of successful business anywhere."

"We do seem to be lilting along almost in defiance of the depression, but people still need clothes and shoes and such." She was relieved to realize that her voice had finally steadied.

He tipped his head, mulling that over. "Just where do you get those clothes and shoes and such?"

"Mainly from manufacturers in Kansas City, where warehouse space costs a lot more than it does here."

"And your orders—where do they come from?"

"The bulk of them come from stores located in large cities. Kansas City, of course, but also St. Louis, Chicago, Omaha. Lately, though, we've received several orders from stores in smaller towns as well."

As she finished her explanation, they arrived at a pair of double swinging doors, one of which had a Blue Eagle poster tacked to it. She crossed in front of him to peer through the dirt-streaked window. A second later she thrust the door open and ushered him forward.

The floor of the warehouse was concrete, the ceiling a network of exposed electrical wiring and water pipes. Tiers of wooden shelves and open bins formed aisles that checkered the cavernous space. A lift truck rumbled in the distance, underscoring the hum of activity as several men shifted items from bins or shelves to boxes and from boxes to bins or shelves. Beneath the hum was a murmur that followed their progress, like a missed beat in the warehouse's pulse. Roxie ignored it as she led Luke to where two men in short-sleeved shirts and denim pants stood in a patch of light swirling with dust motes and cigarette smoke.

"I have a new part-time worker for you, Gary," she said by way of greeting. "Luke Bauer just signed on to fill in when and where you need him."

Tall and thin and a tad stoop-shouldered, the older man squinted thoughtfully at Luke, pressing all the crinkles around his eyes into a new pattern.

The younger one, a stumpy little guy with thick brown brows that formed a single line above his eyes, pulled a hand-rolled cigarette out of his mouth and said, "Bauer?" in a clearly shocked tone.

"That's right, Willie," Roxie confirmed a little too brightly. She turned ever-so-slightly to Luke. "Willie Newcomer here is assistant foreman, while Gary Koch"—she gestured toward the older man, who held several sheets of paper in his hand—"is our head foreman and most indispensable employee."

"Tell many more like that and your nose will be too long for your face." Gary laughed in a low rumble that faintly resembled the idling lift truck.

She laughed, too, and began to relax. Gary teased her only when he was in a good mood. It was his subtle way of letting her know he accepted her decision to hire Luke as a good one.

"Actually," Gary said now, "I could use him full time."

Roxie shouldn't have been surprised, but she was. "Someone else quit?"

"John Corder. Said he couldn't live on what we're paying, so he's packing up Janice and the kids and heading west."

"To California," she said.

"The Promised Land," he scoffed.

"Well, I hope he finds something that suits him."

"He wants to hire on to help build that new Golden Gate Bridge in San Francisco."

She nodded and looked at Luke. "So, does full time work for you?"

Willie's expression turned sour at her question.

Ignoring the acid-faced man, Luke looked at Gary. "When can I start?"

"Tomorrow too soon for you?"

"What time should I report?"

"We start loading the trucks at seven."

"I'll be here at a quarter till." That meant he would have to get up at five in order to eat breakfast and walk the two-plus miles to work, but he would do it and be glad of it.

Hearing his answer, a disgusted Willie stuck the cigarette back in his mouth and stalked away.

"I'll leave Luke with you, Gary," Roxie said. "You can show

him around, explain a bit about his job and such while I speak to Fesol about putting him on the payroll."

She pivoted then and walked out of the warehouse with a pert spring in her step. Even Willie's obvious disapproval couldn't dent her newfound cheer. Gary hadn't raised so much as an eyebrow. In fact, he seemed happy to have replaced a worker without having to go through a lot of rigmarole.

On the other side of the double doors, she stopped and, after the briefest hesitation, she gave in to the urge to look back.

Through the streaks on the windowpane, she watched as Luke removed his worn blue suit coat. He folded it neatly and draped it over his arm with a precision that pleased her. She was a very precise person herself. Not, of course, that that had anything to do with anything.

Even at this distance she could see how much better he looked without that awful old jacket. She could see, too, that he was in excellent shape. His shoulders were broad and his arms were more muscled than she'd have imagined. Not that she'd imagined anything about his muscles, but—

"Are you thinking of cleaning it?" inquired someone behind her.

Roxie started and whirled around, her mouth popping open and her hand flattening on her chest as she came face-to-face with the company's payroll clerk. Tall and gaunt and decked out in his usual work attire of a black suit, white shirt and wide black tie, Fesol Vernal had something of a grim-reaper look about him. He also had an annoying habit of sneaking up on people, which drove her to distraction.

"Fesol!"

"I didn't know you did windows," he said, seeming to tease but failing in the attempt. Fesol wasn't a man given to telling jokes or being joshed and jostled. He was more inclined to accuse than to amuse. And right now he sounded like he was ac-

cusing her of lollygagging.

Squaring her shoulders, she met his accusation with one of her own. "You scared me half to death, sneaking up on me like that."

"I didn't mean . . ." He stopped in mid-apology and glanced from her guilt-stricken face to the window and back again. Then he took a step forward and surveyed the scene through the window. When he turned back, she saw a surge of displeasure, compounded by disbelief, wash over his long, narrow face.

"Don't tell me you hired him," he challenged.

Roxie usually went out of her way to avoid disagreeing with Fesol because arguing with him was like arguing with a brick wall. Once he formed an opinion, he didn't budge from it. This time, though, she had no intention of backing away from a confrontation.

"Yes," she admitted. "I hired him."

He wagged a bony finger at her. "Have you forgotten that he's a convict, a criminal?"

"That was before," she began, but stopped at the short, disgusted sound that Fesol made.

"Do you think seven years in prison made a choirboy out of Bauer?"

"No, but—"

"If you think he's changed, you're more naïve than I'd thought," Fesol went on as if she hadn't spoken. "A leopard doesn't change its spots."

Her chin angled up. "But people do, Fesol. They change all the time, and usually for the better."

He snorted in response.

Remembering how Luke had looked her squarely in the eye when he told her she didn't have to give him a job, Roxie added with emphasis, "The man I interviewed bore very little resemblance to that wild boy everyone remembers. He made no

attempt to excuse or to hide from his past. He simply asked for a job and promised to earn his pay."

As if the sight of her offended her, Fesol removed his steel-rimmed glasses, pulled a precisely-folded handkerchief out of his back pocket and carefully cleaned the lenses. He returned the glasses to his nose, refolded the square of linen along its pressed-in lines and replaced it in his back pocket before speaking again.

"He's probably casing the place, planning to rob us at the first opportunity."

She dismissed that out of hand. "Don't be ridiculous."

"He's robbed before."

"A gasoline station with money in the till, not a—"

"And don't forget that he also stole a car."

"Don't *you* forget that he paid dearly for all of it," she retorted.

Fesol sighed and shook his head in a show of distress. "I knew you'd cause trouble eventually."

"What are you saying?" she demanded in icy tones.

He stepped closer now, crowding her. She either had to tilt her head back to look at him or fall back several steps, which she wasn't about to do. She wasn't going to give an inch of ground.

"I'm saying that the minute I met you I knew you were the type of woman who can't pass by a stray puppy without picking it up and taking it home." He made it sound as if this marked her as a tainted woman.

Squaring her shoulders, she snapped, "Nonsense. It's nothing like that."

"Isn't it?" He took a step backwards, giving her some breathing room. "If you didn't feel sorry for him, why did you hire him?"

Why, indeed? She couldn't deny it. She *had* felt sorry for him

35

and she had hired him for that very reason. Even Luke had re-alized as much. But she couldn't admit it. To do so would seem like a betrayal of him.

She temporized, saying, "Someone has to give him a chance."

"Mr. Stewart should be the one to decide whether or not this company takes such a risk."

Fesol was no longer attacking Luke but her judgment. Some of the strain she felt abated. She was on surer ground, defend-ing herself rather than the man everyone else loved to hate, and she responded with more confidence. "When he hired me, Mr. Stewart explained I'd be making those kinds of decisions whenever he's gone."

"I warned him that was a mistake." Fesol had been here seven years to her seven months, and he rarely missed an opportunity to lord it over her.

She refused to let him rattle her any further. "There's no guarantee that all my decisions will be the right ones, but even if I'm wrong, you aren't the one to object. The decision was my responsibility, not yours."

He opened his mouth, evidently thought better of speaking, and shut it again. Running a hand over his thinning brown hair, he eyed her from behind the thick lenses of his glasses. It wasn't often that someone stood up to Fesol, and it was easy to see that he didn't like it.

Taking advantage of his momentary silence, Roxie spun and left the warehouse area. Try as she might not to, she couldn't help recalling how when Luke walked beside her, the corridor had seemed narrower and her heart had seemed to beat to the rhythm of his movements. Her pulse began to pound now with an intensity that disturbed her. His shadow seemed to haunt her, and though she felt foolish, she couldn't keep from looking back over her shoulder.

Fesol hustled up the hall behind her.

She halted beside the door to her office and waited for him to catch up to her. "Please get Luke Bauer's paperwork ready. He starts work in the morning."

"Of course," the payroll clerk said tightly, and she knew he would. The one thing about him that no one could dispute was that he did his job and he did it well. It was, in Roxie's opinion, the one thing that made him tolerable.

Still, he had to have the last word. "I hope you don't come to regret this."

"So do I," Roxie said in all honesty before stepping into her office and shutting the door behind her.

It wasn't the sanctuary she'd longed for. She couldn't hide from the censorious thoughts that battered her mind. What if Fesol was right? What if she *had* been naïve and trusting, hiring Luke for all the wrong reasons? Even though she could see that he'd changed, she couldn't convince anyone else of it. Only he could do that. And really, it shouldn't be that difficult to do. All he had to do was keep his word and earn his pay.

Sending up a silent prayer that she really had done the right thing, Roxie sat down behind her desk and reached for the stack of orders she'd set aside earlier. She couldn't sit around wringing her hands over this. She had work to do. Whatever her reasons for hiring Luke, she'd made her decision and she would stick by it. If she was wrong . . . well, he might not be the only one out of a job.

# CHAPTER 3

The subtle fragrance of rosewater lingered even after the double doors had swung shut behind Roxie Mitchell. Luke tried to ignore the scent, tried to ignore the stirrings he felt. But after so many years in a world without women, the faint bouquet tantalized him. He wondered what it would be like to immerse himself in the sweetness of it, in the soft, clean sweetness of her.

During their walk from her office to the warehouse, he'd been vividly, painfully aware of her sheer femininity, of the subtle sway of her below-the-knee blue skirt, of her shapely calves, of the strappy white shoes that encased her delicately-boned feet. His response had been immediate and sharp. He managed to suppress the achings. He was well practiced in the denial of his physical needs, but he'd done so only with difficulty. He had never before had to overcome the added allure of a woman's charm.

She had charmed him, all right. She'd charmed him with her kindness, her nervousness, and even with the strength he'd seen in her fine-boned features. She'd charmed him into making that asinine observation about her hair. She'd charmed him into talking, thinking like a regular person. He had been so charmed, in fact, that for a few precious minutes he'd almost forgotten who and what he was.

But Willie Newcomer had brought him back to earth with a jolt, reminding him of exactly who he was: Bauer, the ex-con.

That didn't matter now because he had a job. Relief seeped

in at the realization. Luke savored it, lingering over the delicious taste of it. Unbelievably, he had a job. And with it he had the start to the new life he intended to make for himself.

All he wanted, all he'd dreamed about and longed for these past seven years, was to fade into the normality of life, to work at a steady job, to buy clothes and food, to pay bills and taxes, to just slip into the current of life unconfined by walls. That was all he wanted, all he needed. He didn't expect anything more. He didn't intend to grasp for the brass ring, not this time around.

It was obvious that the foreman and the younger man were surprised that Roxie had hired him. Even more obvious was that the younger one, the one called Willie, was displeased. Luke relaxed a little more. He knew how to deal with Willie. He'd been dealing with the Willies of this world all his life. As for the older one, Luke liked what he saw. He figured he'd get a fair shake. If he did his job, he'd have no trouble from Gary. And he would do his job.

"Hey, Willie," Gary called now to his assistant. "You can check on these orders while I show Bauer around."

Willie visibly hesitated before crossing to his boss, taking the proffered sheets of paper and stamping off. Not seeming to notice his assistant's ire, Gary began outlining the scope of Luke's duties, which mostly entailed filling shipment orders and loading them onto the trucks backed up to the dock. As he listened, Luke looked around the warehouse, instinctively noting the dark corners, the blind spots most likely to lead to trouble. He didn't seem to realize yet that he didn't need to note them. He did it as naturally as he breathed, perhaps more so.

"I'm surprised you don't have men standing in line to work here," Luke commented when Gary wound down.

"A year, even six months ago, we did."

"And now?"

"A number of them have headed for greener pastures."

Luke shot him a puzzled look. "Greener pastures?"

"Just a figure of speech. But there's a group of townsmen who take turns driving into downtown Kansas City every Monday morning to work on the new county courthouse building. They stay in a boardinghouse there during the week and come home on Friday nights.

"Then some of the younger townsmen—as well as a few family men like Corder—have lit out for California in hopes of finding work on the farms or in the oil fields." Gary shrugged. "Can't blame them, I guess. From what I hear it's like paradise, with food just dripping off the trees."

"So how many people work here now?"

"There are ten men, including you and me, in the warehouse. Then there's Fesol Vernal. He's the payroll clerk. And Lana Colomy, the switchboard operator. Vicky Sue Mall, who types up the orders as they come in and the shipping labels for when they go out. Barbara McCanse, Mr. Stewart's secretary—"

"Where does Miss Mitchell fit into the mix?"

"Roxie?" Gary smiled with genuine affection. "I'm not sure what her official title is, but she does a little bit of everything. Bookkeeping. Helping Vicky Sue type up orders. Hiring and firing. Running things when Mr. Stewart is gone."

"Kind of a Jill-of-all-trades, huh?"

"That about sums it up."

They toured the rest of the warehouse, passing a row of wooden lockers and the restroom facilities that were located behind them before ending up in the small cubicle that Gary called his office. It wasn't much bigger than one of those public telephone booths, and it was stuffy and dirty and in total disarray. Empty coffee cups were stacked on a corner of the desk while pencils, in various stages of sharpness, and carbonated copies of shipping orders and other pieces of paper smothered the top. A half-eaten sandwich sat on a wall shelf like the well-preserved artifact of an ancient civilization. It was totally unlike Roxie's office which, while equally small, had been neat and clean and had smelled of her signature rosewater.

"It's a mess," Gary admitted, seeming to read his mind, "but there's a definite order in all this disorganization."

Luke shot him a startled, defensive look. He saw the foreman's grin and realized Gary hadn't really read his mind, that he was simply making small talk. *Small talk?* he thought with shock. He might as well be speaking in a foreign language. Maybe once, in another lifetime, Luke had been able to engage in that sort of idle conversation, but his ability to do so had long since rusted. That he'd done so with Roxie had been an inexplicable aberration, an unguarded instance he didn't intend to repeat lest his reputation rub off on her.

A glimmer of understanding passed through Gary's eyes. He turned and, with a wave of his hand, bid Luke to follow him back out into the warehouse. They continued the tour in silence.

The lunchroom, which also served as the break room for the workers, looked about as drab as the prison's mess hall. A handful of scarred tables topped with overflowing ashtrays and ringed by mismatched chairs were scattered about. On a nearby counter a porcelain coffee pot perked atop a hot plate. A green sugar bowl and a blue creamer sat beside it. The only light in the room came from a bare bulb dangling from a dingy ceiling that might have once been white.

"What's in the icebox?" Luke asked him.

Gary pulled a five-cent piece out of his pants pocket. "Toss a nickel in the basket sitting next to it, and you can pick out a sandwich. And for another nickel you can get a cut of pie or cake."

Luke watched as the foreman paid his money, opened the

icebox door and pulled out a sandwich. "Where does the food come from?"

Gary peeled back the waxed paper, took a bite of the egg salad sandwich he'd selected, chewed, and swallowed before answering. "A local woman makes the sandwiches as well as the pies and cakes, and she stocks the icebox a couple times a week. Then on Friday she and Mr. Stewart split the money in the basket." He gestured toward the hot plate across the room. "The coffee, now that's free."

Luke looked on hungrily as the other man popped the last bite of egg salad in his mouth. He could have used a sandwich himself. It had been a long time since his boarding house breakfast and was a longer time still until supper. But he'd paid a week's rent in advance and was keeping a close watch on what remained of the five dollars he'd received on leaving prison so decided he'd just have to wait.

"C'mon," Gary said as he brushed bread crumbs off the front of his shirt. "I'll show you the dock."

On the concrete dock an operator drove a lone lift truck back and forth, back and forth. It droned on as it loaded boxes of shirts and shoes into the back of a delivery truck. Another truck sat in a different bay. Its driver leaned against the front bumper smoking a cigarette while several other men unloaded a new shipment of boots and socks that had come in from the manu-facturer.

The early May sun slanted fully over all, wrapping Luke and Gary and the workers in warmth. Past the daubing of cars parked willy-nilly out back, a field of wild grass stretched like an expansive, open sea. Luke watched the grass bending in the breeze and knew that, later, he would have the pleasure of walk-ing through it. The knowledge intoxicated him.

"Well, that's about it." Gary, too, looked out over the field. "Any questions?"

"None that I can think of at the moment."

"See you at seven tomorrow morning then," Gary reconfirmed before disappearing back into the maze of the warehouse.

Luke stood motionless on the dock, gripped by a sense of unreality. The grass undulated and beckoned, and he wondered it if was just a mirage, another tantalizing dream from which he'd jolt awake at any moment, the image shattering into fragments of tormented yearning. His stomach clenched and he almost longed for the familiarity of his old cell. It was all so different out here, so jarringly different.

Two weeks ago his physical world had been limited by stone walls and steel bars, a cheerless world of thick air clogged with stale odors, a tedious, colorless routine, an unending monotony twisted by the constant threat of explosive violence. The only time he escaped that depressing place was when he was chained to a long line of other prisoners assigned to do the hot, back-breaking work of pounding rocks into the gravel that would be used for building roads. Now the changing multitude of sights and smells flooded his senses until he feared he'd drown in the deluge.

Funny how you could want something so badly, long for it with every fiber of your being, yet feel your gut tighten with fear when you finally got it. Year after year he'd dreamed of being free again, of coming home to right his wrongs, of finding forgiveness and finally settling down. But on that first walk down Main Street, he'd been keenly aware of the heads that turned toward him and then away. Aware, too, of the whispers and the pointed fingers and the suspicious looks that had followed him down the street. He had wanted to turn around and tell everyone that he'd changed, that all he wanted was a chance to prove it. Yet he kept putting one foot in front of the other, knowing it would be a waste of breath.

He wasn't the only one who'd changed, he had realized as he

looked around the town where he'd grown up. Oh, all the old familiar landmarks like the water tower and the grain elevator and the clock on the spire of the Blue Ridge Fellowship Church remained the same. But the coffee shop where the local farmers had once gathered after morning chores was closed, and the pool hall where he'd wasted so many of his teenage years hustling a game was now a circulating library. And the horses and mules that used to stand rump to rump at the hitching posts had given way to Model T pickups and Brewster wagons.

He hadn't really expected things to be the same after so many years. That didn't even make sense. Yet the changes disturbed him in ways he hadn't foreseen. Each small change seemed to signify a loss of time he'd never be able to recapture.

He felt that same tumbling of emotions now. With all his heart he had wished for a chance to prove himself, a chance to prove that he'd changed. Well, he'd been granted his wish. He had a job and, with it, a chance to make good. Yet fear wrenched at him. A Bauer make good? That was a laugh. The odds were against it, the deck stacked from the day of his birth. He had been set apart long before he even understood what it meant. But from the time he was old enough to realize what was expected of him, Luke had done his best to live up to people's expectations, fulfilling his role as the town's bad boy with due diligence. Once or twice he'd met with unexpected kindness—the general store owners who'd sometimes given him a piece of candy, the third-grade teacher who'd paid for his new school shoes out of her own pocket—but such confusing deeds were few and far between. By the time he was in high school, Luke's fate had been sealed. He was, after all, a Bauer.

Yet something within Luke fiercely rejected this. He'd made a mess of his life, he admitted that, but the past was behind him. The future lay ahead, unblemished. If he'd learned one lesson in all the years of soul-searching, he had learned that he and he alone controlled his own destiny. If it meant swallowing his pride, suppressing his anger, stretching his abilities to their utmost limits, he would do it. He was determined to make a good life for himself.

The knot twisting his stomach loosened. He pivoted on his heel and wound his way back through the warehouse. Willie and another man lounged near the double doors, talking and smoking. They stopped speaking and stared at him stonily as he walked past them. He shoved with extra force, feeling a release in the loud *whoosh* of the doors. There was a newfound sense of power in not having to wait for doors to open at someone else's command.

In something this small did he finally feel he'd regained control of his life.


Practicing a restraint she hadn't known she possessed, Roxie sequestered herself in her office. Though she was eager to learn how Luke was doing, she knew better than to fuss around Gary's domain. She cudgeled her brain but couldn't produce a legitimate excuse for checking in. Without that excuse, all she would do was cause more talk and possibly even trouble. She wistfully eyed the telephone sitting next to her typewriter, hoping in vain for a call from an irate customer whose shipment hadn't been received. The call never came. She stayed in her office.

A surprising amount of work, more than enough to fill her morning, should have kept her occupied. Three new orders had arrived in the mail, a supplier had to be contacted about a shortage of work boots, and next week's work schedule lay in front of her ready to be confirmed and posted. All of this should have made her morning fly, but instead, time trudged along. Minutes plodded like hours and as each dragged by, Roxie found it more difficult to attend to her work. She checked her watch with increasing regularity, feeling restless and trapped.

Her inability to take action only heightened her impatience. She wasn't the type to sit around waiting for someone else to act. If something was missing, she would try to find it. If something was wrong, she would try to set it right. Fix the problem and move on, that was her motto.

But now she felt totally stymied at not being able to march into the warehouse and demand to know how Luke was getting along. Doing so would only give people more food for gossip. Frustrated, she sat at her desk and let her mind travel in circles, returning to the game of second-guessing she'd played most of last night.

Had she taken leave of her senses? Her brother John certainly seemed to think so. Wearing a plaid shirt and a clean pair of overalls, he'd brought his pregnant wife to dinner the night before. No sooner had he heard about what she'd done than he had bluntly told her she had behaved like a "typical woman," thinking with her heart instead of her head.

His wife Lee had been even less help, declaring she thought the whole thing was downright romantic. "You know, like Ramon Novarro as Judah Ben-Hur in *A Tale of the Christ*." Ignoring her husband's incredulous look, she went on, "He comes home and is all alone, with everyone against him. Except *you*, Roxie. You've given him a second chance. And I, for one, think it's . . . noble." She ended on a drawn-out sigh that had caused Roxie to cringe inside.

But it had been her parents' silent concern that disturbed her the most. She'd carried their silence up to bed with her, worrying over it as she had not done over the critical remarks and censorious looks she'd received from others.

Roxie had been blessed. William and Mary Mitchell were loving and giving parents. Their opinion meant a great deal to her. Though all grown up, a full quarter of a century old, she still felt the need for their approval. Even if she'd not seen the flash of concern pass between them, the very fact that they had not expressed an opinion on her action would have told her they disapproved. She could ignore the criticism of the Fesol Vernals and the Agnes Dills. Their objections stemmed from the type of blind prejudice Roxie could neither understand nor accept. But her parents weren't like that. If they thought she'd made a mistake, they had good reason for thinking so. A sadness blanketed her, stifling her in the warm spring night.

She laid awake, regretful, cursing her rashness and wishing she'd not hired him. Already he was fulfilling Marlene's dire prophesy and causing trouble. Throughout her fitful night the question had battered her: *Why* had she done it?

Unfortunately, morning brought no answer. She didn't know why she'd given him a job. Contrary to what her brother and sister-in-law had intimated, the last thing she'd thought of was romance. Fesol had been right. She'd felt sorry for him.

But in the light of a new day that hardly seemed enough of a justification. Her coworkers at Stewart's Warehouse clearly thought she'd lost her mind. She'd seen it in their hurried glances, heard it in their hushed whispers. Maybe they were right. Perhaps her train had slipped off the track. The more she thought about it, the more likely an explanation it seemed. Why else would she have hired Luke Bauer?

She was tired of thinking about it. It was giving her a headache. She glanced at her watch again. The hands finally inched straight up to noon. She grabbed some change out of her clutch purse in the bottom desk drawer and made a grateful escape to the lunchroom.

As she entered, conversation ceased. The chill of unpopularity iced her skin. She knew it would pass, but knowing didn't make it any easier to greet her coworkers. Lana shifted awkwardly on her chair. Vicky Sue looked away. Willie swiped his hand through his matted brown hair before giving her a terse nod. Several others let their eyes slide past hers without recognition.

She opened the icebox door but the sandwich selections blurred before her eyes. Determined not to let their rebuffs upset her any more than they already had, she took a nickel from her skirt pocket and started to put it in the basket. Then she paused as another shiver danced lightly over her. The sensation was quite different from the cold animosity she'd felt before. Curious, she cast a look over her shoulder.

Luke was sitting alone in the far corner, well away from those gathered around the tables in the middle of the room. His face was devoid of any expression. He looked not at her but at the coffee cup in his hands.

Her heart racing, she returned her regard to the sandwiches. She tried to focus on them, but her eyes still refused to co-operate. They were filled with the image of Luke's set face. She tossed her nickel into the basket, reached into the icebox and grabbed a sandwich at random.

Pimiento cheese. She hated pimiento cheese, but there was no putting a sandwich back once it had been unwrapped. A burst of laughter brought her head around. Willie was waving his hands, immersed in one of his tall tales, as the two women sitting at the table next to his listened with smiles of enjoyment. Her annoyance with the pimento cheese transferred instantly to them. They should feel ashamed, ignoring Luke so blatantly, treating him like an outcast. He wasn't a social pariah!

She stole another peek at the far corner. How could they ignore him when his presence charged the very air with a new electricity? His eyes met hers once briefly. She averted her gaze quickly and immediately chided herself. What if he thought he'd offended her just by catching her eye? She turned to the coffee pot perking on the hot plate. Her foot tapped impatiently as she poured herself a cup and added milk until the dark brown brew turned light. The rest of them might have fewer manners than her brother's hogs, but she, at least, had been reared to behave more politely. Collecting her cup, she spun and crossed purposefully to where he sat.

Surprise shot through Luke as he watched her approach. He tensed, unable to look away. The floaty skirt of her flower printed dress swirled about her slender legs with each step she took. The sight of it was enough to stir his imagination. After so many years with nothing but his own mind for stimulation and release, his imagination was incredibly forceful, uncomfortably so. He dropped his gaze and focused his thoughts on the faded denim of the old jeans he planned to replace as soon as he could afford to do so.

She stopped in front of him, the scent of her rosewater further inflaming his imagination. He finished his coffee before finally looking up at her. The corners of her mouth wavered in a tentative smile.

"How has it been going?" she asked, her voice cracking slightly.

"Fine," he said.

"Good. Good." She paused. "That's good," she said again, and fell into silence.

They watched each other, neither one of them speaking nor moving. Roxie began to wish she'd just carried the hated pimento cheese back to her office and eaten at her desk. She could feel the heat of everyone else's stare upon her back, and, worse, the suffocating expectation that hung in the air. It was clearly too late to leave. With all of them observing her so intently, she had to say something, do something.

She cleared her throat. "Do you mind if I sit here?"

He stared at her for a long moment, long enough for her heart to sink all the way to her soles of her T-strap pumps. Why hadn't she left well enough alone? He flicked his gaze to the vacant chair beside him. Then he reached out and wiped the seat with his shirt sleeve.

It was so unexpected, so curiously quaint, that Roxie didn't feel as if she could take a breath or move a muscle, much less actually sit down. When she continued to stand immobile, he said, "If you don't sit, I'll have dirtied my sleeve for nothing."

He was teasing, actually teasing! It affected her in ways she couldn't begin to explore. With every nerve jangling like the firehouse bell, Roxie sat on the just-dusted chair. "Thank you," she said, and instantly wished she hadn't sounded so prim.

"Thank you," he said in return.

She set her sandwich and coffee cup on the table and then swung her gaze to meet his. He looked at her with admiration and an indefinable something else. "Why thank me?" she asked.

"For having the courage to sit with me," he said simply, and that fire bell clanged even louder in her ears.

"Don't be silly," she demurred. "It doesn't take courage to sit with you. Besides, I never do anything courageous. I just wanted to find out how things have been going your first day on the job."

There was no way for him to express the fears, the joys, the raw tangle of emotions he'd been feeling. He shifted. "Okay. Things have been okay."

"Good." Wishing she could think of something more interesting to say, she smoothed out the waxed paper she'd bunched up around her sandwich and rattled on. "I usually bring a sandwich from home and eat it at my desk but I was running late this morning and didn't have time to make one. What did you have?"

He held up his empty cup. "Coffee."

The pimiento cheese remained an inch from her mouth. She gawked at him from over the bread. "That's it? Coffee? Didn't you have a sandwich to go with it?"

"Just coffee." He settled his gaze somewhere in the vicinity of her shoulder. "It's free, and I'm watching the budget until I get that first paycheck."

"I could ask Mr. Stewart to make you a loan from the petty cash fund until then," she offered.

He refused with a quick shake of his head. "I just finished paying my debt to society. The last thing I want is to start out owing my employer."

She dropped her gaze to the bread in her hand, and then thrust it toward him. "Here. Take this. I'll get something else."

"No, I—"

"I insist. You have to eat something. You can't skip a meal when you're working so hard. Besides," she added in all honesty, "you'd be doing me a favor. Really. I hate pimiento cheese. It was a mistake. I picked up the wrong sandwich. Here. Now I can get a ham sandwich. And would you like another coffee?"

He was left holding the pimiento cheese sandwich. She'd jumped up and darted back to the icebox before he could even blink. He knew she was just being kind, sharing with him this way, but such kindness was foreign to him. It had been so long since anyone had cared whether he missed a meal or not, and he didn't quite know how to accept it now.

She returned, handed him another cup of coffee and grinned triumphantly. "I got the last ham sandwich. You don't know how grateful I am to you. I absolutely detest pimiento cheese." She started to sit, but halted in mid-motion. She stared at the uneaten sandwich he still held and her grin vanished. She cast him a look so stricken, it was comical. "Don't *you* like pimiento cheese, either?"

Even if he hadn't, even if eating it would have caused him to break out in boils, Luke would have denied it. As it was, he refuted this with complete truth. "Pimiento cheese is fine."

"Are you sure?"

"I'm sure. In fact, it's one of my favorites." He stretched the truth a little with that last as she continued standing there, a mulish expression he was beginning to recognize coming over her pretty face. Any minute now she'd probably whirl and march to the icebox to get him another sandwich, one more to his liking. Slowly, starting at the corners and gradually working inward, his mouth tilted into a smile. "Now stop gawking and sit down. A man can't eat when he's being stared at."

That crooked curve of his lips dazzled Roxie. It transformed him completely. Years washed away, distrust dissolved, severity vanished. She managed to plop down as he took a huge bite of the sandwich. They ate in silence, both aware they were being keenly observed. Subdued bits of conversation drifted over them, and Roxie struggled to find something to say. But she couldn't tell him how breathtaking she found his smile. She couldn't tell him how much better, how much younger and more fit he looked in the jeans and blue work shirt instead of that horrid old suit. As she wiped the last crumbs from her lips, she decided work was the most appropriate topic.

"So, do you think you'll like the work here?"

"I'd like working anywhere the air smelled free," he said.

She tossed a startled look his way. She wanted to say something deep and meaningful, something to let him know how much she was touched by him. All she managed was another inane, "Good," which sounded so hollow and stupid to her ears, she decided she would do best to excuse herself and leave. She started to rise but happened to glimpse Willie's face. He glared at Luke with unmistakable hostility.

Annoyed, Roxie turned a bright smile to Luke. "I'm certain you'll like it even more once you've gotten used to the routine. And, of course, once everyone's gotten used to you."

His long lashes lowered. He studied her from beneath them. For no logical reason her heart gave a little bump.

"You mean once they've gotten used to an ex-con?" he asked on a drawl that held a tinge of menace. Or perhaps it was a twinge of pain.

Her brows drew together. She searched his expression, trying to decipher what, exactly, his tone had conveyed. His eyes were carefully void, his mouth an indefinable line, his cheekbones angularly set. She would not discover the answer that way. He was closed to her.

"Yes, I suppose in a way I do mean that," she said slowly. His jaw tightened and her heart twisted. "But what I really mean is once they've realized you're more than that. Once they've gotten to know you as a person, things will even out."

His distrust was plain for her to see. He didn't believe her, and she didn't know how to convince him otherwise. She didn't know why it was so important to her that he believe her. But it was important, heartstoppingly important, that she make him believe.

"Luke, I realize it isn't easy for you," she began in an earnest tone. "I know it can't be. But try to understand that it's not easy for us either. You've got to give us a little time—"

"I've done my time," he cut in, his voice clipped.

She drew in a sharp breath. Luke saw the hurt cross her features and hated himself for it. Then he saw the pity that immediately followed and hated her for that.

Chairs scraped back, grating against the silence between them. One by one, the other diners ambled away, leaving only the echoes of their chatter. Roxie watched Willie hover by the door, willing him not to go, but he stayed only long enough to enjoy a seductive swish of Vicky Sue's departing skirt. Then she and Luke were alone.

Roxie counted each frantic beat of her heart, trying to find something to say amid the tumbling of embarrassment and compassion she felt. At length, she forced herself to look at him.

His austere expression didn't invite apologies or commiserations. But she had to say something. She couldn't go on sitting there like a lump of lead.

After an eternal moment she jerked to her feet. "I guess I should get back to work."

"Wait," he said, the same thing she'd said to him the day he'd applied for work.

She hesitated.

Luke glanced around the empty room, finally bringing his gaze to rest on her face. He had no idea what to say. He just knew he couldn't let her walk out on such a negative note.

"Yes?" she prompted.

Rising, he stood next to her.

Roxie tipped her head back to look up at him. His black hair glowed with a clean sheen while the scar on his cheek shone whitely against his tanned skin. She saw his pulse beating furiously against his temple and felt an urge to soothe it with her fingertips. She took a step away from him, away from his magnetic force, before she did something she would live to regret.

Luke read rejection in her hasty movement. Nothing in his life had ever seemed as important as regaining her acceptance, and he spoke with quiet urgency. "I'm sorry. After so much time waiting, I guess I've gotten impatient. I know acceptance won't come easily, from them or from me."

"From you?"

"It's not easy for me to accept being an ex-con," he admitted. Before she could give way to another burst of pity, he crooked his lips in that uneven smile and said, "Anyway, I never did thank you yesterday for the job."

Like sunshine spilling from behind clouds, her smile suddenly brightened the room. "Oh, you needn't thank me for that."

"I want to. I want you to know I appreciate what you've done for me."

"I haven't done anything. It's what you'll do that matters."

"But you've given me the chance."

Happiness gripped her, squeezing her until it was almost painful. It crushed the breath from her, and Roxie didn't have enough left to speak another word. It was just as well. She wouldn't have known what to say anyway. Giving him another smile, she again turned to leave.

"And Miss Mitchell," he said, halting her.

She looked over her shoulder. Her heart nearly stopped. His eyes were flashing like quicksilver.

"I won't let you down," he promised.

She left the lunchroom feeling as if she were walking on air.

# CHAPTER 4

The irate clothing store owner called a week later. As was usual in the case of missing shipments, Roxie referred the caller to Gary. As was not usual, she followed it up the next morning with a personal visit to his office. When she didn't find him there, she went in search of him through the labyrinth of the warehouse.

Though her view was partially blocked by stacks of new boxed merchandise waiting to be sorted into the various bins, she had no trouble locating the foreman. His silvery hair stood out like a beacon in the dim light, and she strode forward, passing two pickers who were packing up boxes of work boots for shipment. As she'd known it would, the chilly reserve was melting, and she received several friendly greetings along the way.

"Good morning, Gary," she called as she neared.

He nodded absently, continuing to study an inventory sheet he held. Knowing better than to interrupt him, she waited quietly, letting her eyes wander in the interim. She wasn't consciously searching through the warehouse canyons, yet there was a definite sense of accomplishment when her gaze came to rest on Luke.

His back was to her as, unaware of her presence, he removed a strapped box from a heavy-duty scale, marked the weight on the top and shoved it aside. In deference to the heat he'd rolled up the sleeves of his blue cambric shirt, but there were damp circles underneath his armpits and the back of it was soggy with sweat. When he reached for another box, the wet material stretched tightly across his back, delineating each vertebra and emphasizing the musculature. The sight of it caused her heart to knock against her ribs.

He paused between boxes to swipe his arm across his brow. The same sweat that beaded in his dark hair now glistened on his forearm. Even in repose there was no mistaking the strength of those arms. What would it be like to be held in them? Her mouth went dry, and her breath clogged in her throat at the thought of being wrapped within the powerful circle—

"Roxie," Gary prompted.

She returned to reality with a jolt and swung her startled gaze to the foreman. As she focused on him, she had the sinking feeling it wasn't the first time he'd spoken her name. A bristling irritation quickly chased away her embarrassment. What was the matter with her? She was acting like a complete fool!

"What brings you back to the warehouse?" Gary asked a shade impatiently.

She could see he would consider talking with her a waste of time, but now that she was here, she had to say something. She plunged in. "I just wondered if you'd solved yesterday's problem—the lost order for Lasater's Clothing Store in El Dorado, Kansas. Did you ever find out what happened?"

If Gary thought her inquiry odd, he didn't show it. "The order never got out of the warehouse," he told her. "We didn't have a shipping slip on it, and I was about to chew Willie's—tell Willie to find out what had happened when Luke found the slip stuck behind one of the bins."

Involuntarily her gaze veered to Luke. He moved with an economy of motion, a supple strength that mesmerized her. How long she stared at him she didn't know, but it was long enough for the silence to strike her, long enough for her to realize Gary had followed the direction of her stare. He was eyeing Luke with speculation, and she winced mentally.

"Luke found the slip, you said?" she asked, striving for an offhand tone.

Gary shot her a sharp look. "Yeah. It must've fallen off a pile of cartons or gotten misplaced or something. Just one of those things that happens. Mr. Stewart had us ship out a couple of extra shirts, gratis, to make up for it. The whole load went out this morning."

"Well, I'm glad it all got straightened out." She knew she should leave. She'd used up her meager excuse, but still she lingered. Gary, too, waited, seeming to expect something more. Feeling awkward, unsure in a way she'd not felt since adolescence, she finally brought herself to ask, "How's he doing, by the way?"

Gary didn't pretend not to understand. "Does his job and keeps to himself."

She could have shaken him until his teeth rattled. She wanted details, descriptions, something to point to the next time she talked to Fesol so she could say, *See? I told you he'd make it.* Instead, Gary gave her a laconic pat on the head.

"Still, in a week, you must've seen whether or not he does a good job," she persisted.

"Good enough."

She gave up. You couldn't pry anything out of Gary Koch he didn't want you to have. Saying she was glad the snafu with Lasater's had been straightened out, she left him. Threading her way along the aisles of towering shelves, she decided her short visit hadn't been totally wasted. At least she could be buoyed by the fact that Luke was doing okay. "Good enough" was about as much praise as anyone could expect from Gary.

"Keeps to himself," he'd also said. Roxie didn't have to wonder what that meant. Given what had happened in the lunchroom the day she ate with Luke, she could be fairly certain that the others were still ignoring him. She could only guess at this because she hadn't had the courage to return after that day, choosing instead to bring her lunch from home and eat at her desk or, on particularly nice days, to take her sandwich outside to the wooden picnic table that sat on the east side of the warehouse. It was too risky to go back. He'd disturbed her too much and in ways she didn't want to examine too closely.

Her lips began to tighten. She was being absurd. All they'd done was talk a little bit. And really, if she wanted to know how Luke was doing, she should simply ask him. She was behaving foolishly, avoiding him. He might even misinterpret it. After all, there was no doubt about why everyone else avoided him.

Roxie halted in her tracks. No, she wasn't going to treat him the way everyone else did. People made mistakes, she knew that only too well, and she wasn't going to condemn his future along with his past, not unless she had reason to do so.

She smoothed the skirt of her pink shirtwaist dress and combed her fingers through her hair. She would simply ask him how he was, chat a bit, and then get back to work. Breathing in deeply, she retraced her steps.

"Good morning, Luke," she said, and congratulated herself on her level tone of voice.

He spun around, wary surprise crossing his face. It passed swiftly, leaving a guarded pleasure. "Good morning, Miss Mitchell."

"Please, call me Roxie. We're all on a first-name basis around here."

He nodded, but he didn't say it. A few seconds thudded by, seconds in which she learned just how much she would have liked to have heard her name on his lips. He leaned against the scale, his pose deceptively casual. She knew the pose was misleading. Nothing about him was ever casual. Not daring to ask herself why, she wished she could erase his tension.

"Gary says your work's good enough," she finally said. "Coming from Gary, that's high praise indeed."

He nodded again but didn't smile or show any other kind of emotion. "I'm glad to hear it. I think a lot of Gary's opinion."

"We all do." She waited, hoping he would say something more. When he didn't, she shuffled the toe of her white shoe over the bare concrete and gathered her courage together. "Maybe we could have lunch again sometime," she suggested in a voice that sounded disgustingly squeaky to her own ears. To cover her embarrassment, she added in a teasing tone, "You owe me one."

"Sounds good," he said, but there was an unconvincing quality about his agreement.

Roxie wanted to press him, to name a day, and have him commit to it, but she sensed his discomfort and let it drop. Saying good-bye, she was about to move on when she caught sight of two pickers watching her with intent interest. They exchanged a comment, and the blatant derision in their expressions nettled her.

She wanted to lash out at them, to tell them to get back to work, but that would probably make things worse for her and for Luke. Instead, she impulsively exclaimed, "I'm sorry for the way they're all behaving."

Luke gaped at her with open incredulity. He couldn't imagine anyone feeling that much concern on his behalf, especially not someone like Roxie. She was so obviously everything he wasn't, so good, so upright, so pure.

"You don't have to apologize for anything—" he started.

"Yes, I do!" she interrupted fiercely. "They haven't the manners to do it, so I will. It's shameful the way they ignore you."

Her outburst stirred too many emotions in him. He'd worked at being insensate for so long, he didn't know how to handle such feelings. Normally he'd resist them with a detached indifference, but he couldn't even pretend indifference to her.

Mustering a reasonably light tone, he contradicted her. "But I haven't been ignored."

She cast him a look of disbelief that changed instantly to one of sheer fury. "If anyone's been haranguing you—"

"No, I didn't mean anything like that," he broke in quickly. "All I meant was that they've been watching me, not ignoring me. Most days, I've practically had my own shadow."

"Shadow," she echoed.

"I think his name is Fesol." Crinkling his gray eyes in a smile, he beguiled her into forgetting her fuming indignation. When he looked at her like that, it was a wonder she could remember her own name.

"I'd call him something a whole lot less polite than a shadow," she returned with an answering smile and had the pleasure of hearing him chuckle.

"But you're a lady, so you'll courteously refrain from doing so," he joked.

Her smile slowly faded. She wasn't such a lady, but she couldn't bear the thought of him knowing it. She could scarcely stand to admit it to herself. He might be able to openly bear the stigma of his past—it was one of the things she most admired about him—but she couldn't. Not yet, at least. As quickly as she could politely do so, Roxie told him she'd hold him to that lunch one day and strode off through the warehouse maze.

The raucous noise surrounding her seemed to mimic the clamor of her confused emotions. Once again, without even trying, he'd managed to thoroughly unsettle her. Even Arthur hadn't run her through such a gamut of emotions. She'd felt sorry for Luke, angry on his behalf, saddened by her own secretive past. But most of all she had felt attracted to him. She couldn't deny it. It would be useless to try. She still tingled from seeing him smile. But before she'd even spoken to him

61

today, she'd felt it. She'd been carried away by the mere sight of him.

*Slow down, Roxie,* she warned herself. *This isn't the sort of man for you to tangle with without a lot of thought.* Being concerned about the employee was one thing. Being concerned about the man was something else again. She hadn't come home from St. Louis simply to jump from the frying pan into the fire. Resolving to put Luke Bauer out of her mind, she headed for her office.

Barbara McCanse, Mr. Stewart's secretary, intercepted her in the corridor, holding one palm up and one palm out. "Wait a minute, Roxie. Do you have a nickel I can borrow? I'd like to get a piece of pie, but I'm too lazy to go all the way back to my desk to get my purse."

"Sorry, but my purse is in my desk, too."

Barbara's pretty face wrinkled in a comical mixture of disappointment and acceptance. "Some panhandler I'd make. Oh well, I guess the exercise will do me good," she drawled, patting her hips and grinning as she fell into step beside Roxie.

"I'm sorry I couldn't help."

"That's okay," Barbara said with a shrug. "I should have figured your purse would be locked up too. Isn't it a bother?"

Roxie threw her a puzzled glance. "Isn't what a bother?"

"You know, locking our purses in our desk drawers." Barbara frowned. "Don't you keep yours locked up?"

"No, I don't."

"Oh."

"Since when have you started doing that?" Roxie asked, feeling that angry prickle crawl under her skin.

"Well, you know," Barbara wriggled uncomfortably under Roxie's steady glare. "I mean, you've got to admit, it doesn't hurt to take precautions."

"Whose idea was this?"

Barbara gawked at the furious flush on Roxie's face. "Well, um, you know—"

"No, I don't know. That's why I'm asking. Who told you to lock up your purse?"

"Fesol," Barbara said with a downward twitch of her mouth. "He said he wouldn't leave them out anymore if he were us and really, it just made sense . . ."

Roxie didn't hear Barbara's words wither into nothingness. She had already wheeled and marched in the direction of the main office. All her earlier indignation returned, centralized on one person. Fesol was the one who hadn't wanted to give Luke a chance. Fesol was the one hounding him now. Fesol was the one instilling nasty, vicious ideas in everyone else's head. Roxie felt like strangling Fesol, but she contented herself with slamming into Layton Stewart's office and insisting that something be done.

Sitting behind his desk, he looked up from the circular he'd been studying with a flicker of concern for the frosted glass rattling in his just-slammed door. "Done about what, Roxie?"

"Fesol!"

"Fesol?"

"Fesol Vernal," Roxie clarified through clenched teeth. "Fesol Vernal and his snake-in-the-grass tactics!"

Layton Stewart was a friendly-looking man with pomaded silver hair, wire-rimmed spectacles, and a ready smile. Now a slow version of that smile started at the edges of his mouth and worked its way up to his hazel eyes. Roxie stood shaking in front of his desk, unable to speak for fear of shocking him with language no one would ever suspect she knew.

"I don't think," he remarked at last, "that I've seen anything quite like this since that tornado flattened Hector McKenzie's barn back in twenty-eight."

"This isn't funny, Mr. Stewart."

63

"Well, then, suppose you sit down and tell me what 'this' is so I can appreciate the seriousness of it all."

Roxie looked mutinous for a fraction of a second, then plopped into the straight-backed chair beside his desk and took a deep, steadying breath before letting the words pour out. "You backed my decision on hiring Luke Bauer, which I truly appreciated, and I think you'll agree now that we have to do what we can to help him adjust here. And that means putting a stop to Fesol's interference. He's undermining any chance Luke has of gaining people's trust."

"Is that so?"

When her employer used that tone, Roxie felt about four years old. She bit her lip and went on more slowly. "Fesol's not only been watching everything Luke does, which influences others to do the same, he's also told Barbara and the other women to lock their purses in their desks. That sort of advice engenders distrust."

"And what exactly do you recommend we do to stop this insidious fiend?"

"Mr. Stewart! I'm serious."

Hooking his thumbs under his trademark red suspenders, he sat back in his chair and eyed Roxie over the tops of his spectacles. "I don't like this sort of thing any more than you do, Roxie. But I can't fire Fesol for being Fesol any more than I would fire Luke for being 'that wild Bauer boy.' "

"I wasn't suggesting you fire Fesol—"

"No, but there's not much of anything else I can do," he pointed out. "I can't tell him to quit being suspicious. He'd just think me a naïve old fool."

A rueful smile touched Roxie's lips. "He's as much as told me I'm a young one."

"If people want to listen to Fesol and keep their valuables under lock and key, who are we to say they're wrong? If it makes them feel better, can we really demand they don't do it?"

She had no answer for him so she just sat there and waited for him to continue.

"I think you should let time take care of these things," he counseled.

"You think Luke will be all right?" she asked in a quiet tone.

He nodded with the same decisiveness that had made him such a successful businessman. "Luke Bauer strikes me as a man who's perfectly capable of taking care of himself."

Roxie didn't know if she believed him. Luke seemed so lost somehow, like a soul without a home. She ached inside just thinking about it. But she also recognized the sense behind Mr. Stewart's words. She could see that her own interference wasn't any better than Fesol's. Silently vowing not to stick her nose into it anymore, she smiled at her employer and started to rise.

"Hold your horses a minute," he told her. "I've given you my opinion. Now I'd like to have yours." He picked up the one-page advertising circular that he'd been looking at when she slammed into his office and handed it to her. "I got this in the mail the other day, but I just now got around to looking it over today."

Roxie studied the front and saw it was from a Kansas City dress manufacturer.

"What do you think of those calico cloth housedresses on the back?"

She turned the circular over to look at them. "The rickrack around the neck and on the pockets is a nice touch."

"Do you think they'd sell in the dry goods stores we supply?"

And thoughts of Luke fled as Roxie returned her attention to business.

She wasn't even thinking about him when she saw him. Carrying the cloth lunch bag her mother had made her, she was headed toward the picnic table on the east side of the warehouse where she planned to eat her sandwich when she happened to glance out over the field beyond the parking lot. A lone figure was stretched out in a small clearing in the grass. She paused in mid-stride, feeling uncertain about disturbing his solitude. Then she impulsively struck out across the field and strode toward him.

As she neared, her gait slowed to a hesitant walk. His dark hair shone like a raven's wings in the sunlight as he lay with his hands stacked beneath his head. Disappointment nipped at her heels. He was sleeping. She shouldn't bother him. About to turn back, she halted when he opened his eyes, caught sight of her and sat up.

"I didn't mean to disturb you," she hurriedly explained.

"You're not." That wasn't quite truthful, Luke thought. She always disturbed him, though it was as pleasurable as it was painful.

"It's such a pretty day that I decided to eat my lunch outside," she explained, holding up the bag she carried from home. "Would you like to join me?"

"Thanks, but I already ate." He'd made himself a bacon sandwich from the leftovers of his boardinghouse breakfast and had brought it with him to work. "Besides," he added on a mellow chuckle, "I still owe you a lunch."

"That's right, you do." Her voice took on a teasing lilt.

"All I can offer you now, though, is water." He picked up a capped glass jar that looked to be about half-full and shook it.

"How about a seat?"

"A what?"

"If you won't join me, may I join you?" She didn't wait for his answer but handed him the bag containing her sandwich and an apple and then sank to the ground beside him.

Watching her tuck her blue striped cotton skirt around her

legs, Luke could barely control the flood of sensations that threatened to drown him whenever she was near. For once he was grateful for the long years of practice at hiding his true feelings. At least he could keep her from seeing how affected he was.

"Here you go," he said when she was settled.

"Thanks." Smiling, she reached for her bag.

Their fingertips grazed as she took it back. Their eyes met, each mirroring shock as an unlabelled emotion arced between them. She lowered her gaze. He dragged his away just as quickly.

Roxie's lunch lay forgotten in her lap as she waited for her heart to steady and her breathing to return to normal. When it had, she said, "Do you come out here often?"

"Every day. I like to be out in the open." His mouth crooked in a rueful smile. "And the lunchroom reminds me too much of places I'd rather forget."

A gentle breeze cavorted through the grass, but it didn't cool the heated curiosity building inside Roxie. She had to know. She had to hear it straight from him. Into the charged silence she blurted out, "What happened, Luke? What went wrong?"

"I got caught," he said, his voice flippant.

"Please don't," she pleaded.

"You know what happened. Everybody does." Repressed emotion roughened his voice.

"I was away at school when you left," she told him. "I never really knew all the details."

"And you haven't asked anyone?"

"I wanted to hear it from you."

Luke shifted restlessly. He had known it would come to this. Sooner or later it always came back to this. His past oppressed his life. But if he were ever to come to an understanding with Roxie, it couldn't be avoided. As much as he dreaded it, he had to try to explain. But what should he say? If he said too much, she might think he was making excuses. Too little, and he might not convince her how much he regretted his past mistakes. What to say? How to begin?

He crossed his legs Indian-style and stared out over the flat horizon. Just grass and sky with nothing in between. As always, the view soothed him. Finally, he began at the beginning.

"I was what went wrong," he said matter-of-factly. "My parents never really wanted me. I was just an accident, or so I was always told, and each blamed the other for me. My mother deserted us before I was even five. My old man was a drunk whose favorite pastime was beating me—while I was still small enough not to fight back, that is." He paused. "You know, my father never once said he loved me," he added, dropping his voice a decibel.

He didn't look at her, which Roxie thought was probably just as well. She knew she was one of those people whose faces reflected what they were feeling, and what she was feeling right now was a deep sadness for the little boy whose parents had never hugged him or kissed him or held him in loving arms. He didn't want anyone's pity. He'd made that clear the day she hired him. So she locked her grief inside, where her soul rocked with suffering for him.

"No one except Granddad Marchand—my mother's father— ever seemed to expect anything of me," he continued. "I pretty much grew up thinking I had to take on everyone in sight. Take them before they took me. All I ever really wanted was out. Out from under my father's fists, out of Blue Ridge, out of the life I was leading. But I was mired in it. I knew what people thought of me, and I did my best to reinforce their opinion, directing all my energy to being *the* Bauer to end all Bauers. More and more I followed my father's footsteps, drinking and fighting and wasting my life. As strange as it sounds, I think he finally approved of me."

Luke risked a glance her way. Her head was bent, her face veiled by a honey-colored fall of hair. He was almost relieved he couldn't see her reaction. He couldn't bear to see her disbelief, her distaste, her disgust. Hoping with all his being that she wouldn't hate him for what he'd done, he forced himself to go on.

"I'd had an ongoing feud with the owner of the gasoline station."

"Buck Roberts."

"Right." He plucked a blade of grass and chewed on it, gathering his thoughts. "Old Buck was always egging me on, calling me a crumb and a bum and a raft of other names I won't repeat. Then one day he said some things about my parents. Now he didn't say anything about them that I hadn't thought or said myself over the years, but I took exception to *him* saying them."

He shook his head in self-deprecation. "I'd been drinking, of course, and decided I'd just have to teach the old codger to have a little more respect."

Roxie crossed her arms over her stomach as if it pained her. Tightly she clasped her elbows with the opposite hands. She couldn't lessen her grip. She felt if she let go, she'd let go of her control and throw herself against him in a burst of tears.

"So you robbed him," she said, her voice breaking slightly.

Anger, fear, even a rare touch of self-pity, gnawed at Luke, and he spouted out, "Keep in mind that I was a twenty-year-old kid with a chip on my shoulder and a grudge. I was drunk and angry, but even while I was in the act of taking my grandfather's gun out of the drawer he kept it in, even when I was in the act of robbing that station, I was regretting it. A thousand times I've wished I could go back and change it all. If I could, God knows I would. But I can't. I can't change the past."

"I know that!" Roxie cried. She'd been afraid to say anything more than she already had, but she could no longer remain silent. She'd hurt him. And in hurting him, she'd pained herself unbearably. "I'm sorry, Luke. I didn't mean to stir up old wounds. What happened then doesn't matter now."

"Oh, yes, it does," Luke countered through gritted teeth. "It matters every time I see someone avoid me. It matters every time I realize how much of my life I wasted. It matters every time I remember how deeply I disappointed my grandfather, the only person who ever really believed in me."

He dragged in a deep, cleansing breath and let it out slowly before he went on. "But if I can't change the past, I can change the man. And believe me, I've changed."

"I know you have," she said more calmly. "That's why I wanted to hear your side of it. What you did then didn't seem to match up with the man I know you are now. I wanted to understand it. Thank you for explaining."

Relief flooded through him, lightening and lifting him. She didn't hate him. She didn't even think less of him. "You don't need to thank me. I wanted to explain. I wanted you to know that I'm trying to turn things around. I'm living up to my own expectations now, no one else's, and I expect myself to make good."

His voice trailed away like one of those clouds he liked to watch and he gave a humorless laugh. "It's so easy to go wrong and so hard to make it all right."

"How many men even try?" she questioned softly.

Ironing all expression from his face, Luke came abruptly to his feet. Once again, Roxie had stirred up emotions he hadn't thought he still possessed. He felt wrung out and more than a little vulnerable. He hated to admit it, but he couldn't deny that his past mattered. It mattered way too much. He spent every day of his life facing up to that fact. He couldn't believe she would be able to disregard it in the long run.

Uncertainty replaced his fading relief. After she'd thought about it a bit, he felt sure she'd realize what a mistake it would be to get involved, however innocently, with him. And he didn't think he would be able to bear the pain of her inevitable rejection.

So he did what he had to do. He retreated behind the defensive aloofness that had served him so well of late and said coolly, "I've bored you long enough. Besides, we've got to get back to work."

By the time Roxie got to her feet, he had turned and stalked away. Appetite gone, she held her unopened lunch bag and tried to digest what she had just learned about Luke. She wanted to run after him and tell him that he hadn't bored her in the least. She wanted most of all to assure him that she believed in him. But realizing that he probably wouldn't stop to listen, she blew out a discouraged breath and followed him back to the warehouse.

# CHAPTER 5

May melted away into June in a heat wave that wrung out the town and worried the surrounding farmers. "It's gotta rain soon" was a continual refrain heard from the bank to the blacksmith's to the barber shop. News that poor Phil Campbell had gone under brought a nodding of heads and a round of speculation as to who would be the next to lose his farm or his business. As the heat wave progressed, scarcely anyone remembered to be concerned over having Luke Bauer back in town. In fact, except for a few speculative looks tossed his way after Kansas City's bloody Union Station Massacre was plastered all over the front page of the newspaper, scarcely anyone even seemed to remember he was in town at all.

Luke welcomed the quiet neglect. It was preferable to the mute animosity he'd received upon his return and it bestowed upon him the freedom that comes with anonymity. After years of sharing his cell with hardcore criminals, of listening to other prisoners hollering at each other and at the guards, of never having a moment to himself, he relished the solitude.

On his way back to the boardinghouse at the end of a work day, he often cut through the open field, enjoying the clean air and reveling in the boundless view. Sometimes he'd sprawl in the grass, hands beneath his head and watch the puffy white clouds floating across the vast blue sky. Eventually his eyes would drift closed and he would remember the pretty flower printed dress and how its full skirt had swirled around Roxie's legs as she'd walked toward him in the lunchroom his first day on the job.

He could feel himself getting all worked up, just thinking about it, and he vowed to quit thinking about it, about her, about the two of them. It was a waste of time to be losing himself in hopeless fantasies like that. She was good and pure and everything he wasn't. He'd made his decision, the only decision he could have made, and he'd stuck to it.

Other than a couple of brief, unavoidable conversations, Luke had kept his distance from Roxie. Whenever she came into the warehouse, which seemed to be less and less frequently these days, he'd found reasons to busy himself elsewhere. Though at first she'd tried to draw him out, reminding him of the lunch she was due and teasing him about his excuses, she eventually quit pressuring him. He told himself he was glad she had, but that wasn't true and he knew it.

Loneliness was no stranger to him. He'd lived with it most of his life. He knew, or thought he knew, how to live with the isolation. But over these past couple of months the empty hours had become longer, the barren days bleaker. At times he could feel despair eating away at him, wearing him down, corroding his determination to continue walking the straight and narrow. So far, though, he'd managed to stay the course.

Now, he jotted a note in the shipping log and reminded himself that he didn't need anyone else. His parents were long gone, and, to his everlasting regret, his grandfather had died while he was in prison. No, he had only himself and that was just fine. He liked being alone—or so he told himself.

He glanced up and realized that he was just that, alone. The warehouse had emptied out a half hour earlier. He'd stayed on to finish filling out the log and had wasted his time daydreaming instead. Closing the log with a snap, he took it into Gary's office and laid it atop the disorganized pile on his desk. Then he switched off the lights and made his way back through the darkened warehouse. His eyes adjusted easily, and his stride was long and confident as he walked through the now-familiar aisles. As he neared the exit, he quickened his step and rounded the last corner.

He smacked into someone. Felt the bone-jarring impact. Heard a smothered exclamation. Saw a silhouette tumble backward.

Luke shot out his arms, but grasped only air as Roxie crashed into a pillar of cartons that had yet to be loaded onto the trucks. The cardboard shaft wobbled, then toppled. Boxes pitched in all directions, landing with thuds and thumps all around him. He heard her land with a resounding *thwack* and her cry of pain rang in his ears.

He knelt, his heart pounding wildly. "Oh, my God, are you hurt?"

Roxie sat perfectly still, gawking up at him in disbelief and wishing one of the boxes had knocked her unconscious. She hated knowing she must look like a complete idiot, sitting there with her arms and legs splayed, the skirt of her dimity dress hiked up around her knees, and her hair falling down into her eyes. It didn't help that her mouth was hanging open, either, so she clamped it closed and tried to recover at least a semblance of composure.

"Are you hurt?" he repeated, his voice gruff. "Should I call a doctor?"

Pushing her hair out of her face with both hands, she offered a wobbly smile. "No, I'm fine. I mostly just had the breath knocked out of me."

"Are you sure?"

His obvious anxiety surprised her. After the way he'd steered clear of her recently, she'd figured he would care more about the crushed boxes than about her. "Well, I think so," she said cautiously. "I probably bruised my dignity more than anything."

To prove her point, she picked up the clutch purse she'd dropped when she fell and tried to scramble to her feet. Needles of pain flashed up her right shin and her spine. She teetered for a few seconds and then sank like the setting sun beneath the toppled cartons.

He grabbed her, easing her backward tumble. "You *are* hurt," he said in an accusing tone.

Making a pained face, she nodded and pointed down at her right leg. "My ankle."

He followed the direction of her extended finger past her exposed calf to the small turn of her ankle. He swallowed dryly. Ah, the hours he'd spent visualizing her legs! With an effort, he assumed the most virtuous bedside manner he could manage and cupped her ankle in his hand. His fingertips were warm, his touch surprisingly gentle as he probed her swollen ankle, but still she winced.

"You've definitely given it a bad wrench." It struck him that she was fragile, as delicate as china. She could have broken the bone so easily. Something within him constricted at the thought. "I'm sorry," he said again. "I'm so sorry. I never meant to run you down. You're the last person in the world I'd ever want to hurt."

An inner tingling dwarfed Roxie's physical aches. It seemed to radiate from where his fingers encircled her ankle, searing all the way through her silk stocking and her skin. "Don't be silly," she said shakily. "It was as much my fault as yours. I was rushing to leave and I wasn't watching where I was going."

The gnarl within Luke's gut uncoiled. His strained muscles eased. He'd been blamed for mistakes all his life, yet the one time he was willing to accept all the blame, she wouldn't let him. He looked at the pinch of pain upon her features and wished he could absorb all her hurt as easily as she absorbed his.

"I think I'd better get a doctor," he decided.

"There's no need for that. It's just a sprained ankle. I've done this before. Honest." She flashed a mouthful of gleaming white teeth at him. "I'll be good as new in no time."

"But we ought to do something," he persisted. "I can already see the swelling."

"I just need to soak it in ice water," she told him. "Maybe you could chip some off the block in the lunchroom icebox. Then after I've soaked it a bit and the swelling goes down, I can drive on home."

Luke scanned the shadowed warehouse and knew it would be impossible. It was too dark, too deserted. If even one person ever learned that she'd stayed there alone with him, her reputation would be in shreds. *His* reputation would guarantee that. No one would ever believe the sprained ankle was anything but a cover. Old-fashioned as it seemed, he couldn't compromise her.

He removed his hand and said tonelessly, "It would be better if you went straight home."

Her ankle was throbbing more violently now and Roxie had begun to realize that her bottom felt like a dented fender. He was giving her that remote look she hated, and she decided she'd like nothing better than a good cry. In a voice laden with unshed tears, she contradicted her earlier statement. "I can't drive almost three miles with a sprained ankle."

"We could call your parents or one of your brothers," he suggested.

Roxie wouldn't have thought it possible to feel so stung by rejection. After Arthur, she'd thought she was immune to that sort of pain. But obviously she'd been wrong. Luke didn't want her intruding in his life, not even for a few minutes. It shouldn't have hurt. He'd made his feelings clear long before this. But it did hurt, terribly, and the tears she'd been fighting spurted forth now in a gigantic sob.

Instantly alarmed, he reached for her. "Oh, God, please don't cry."

She blindly thrust his hands away. "You don't need to bother about me." She contradicted herself yet again, gasping between sobs, "I'll drive myself home. It's only three miles."

"Don't be ridiculous," he chastised her, all business now. "Stop crying and let me help you up."

With a defiantly loud sniff she allowed him to ease her up with her weight on her left foot.

Luke steadied her as she gained her balance, his heart slamming in his chest when she leaned a hairbreadth away from him. He knew he should let her go, find a chair to deposit her in and run to the warehouse telephone to call for help. But his senses soared and filled with wonder as he lingered over the satin smoothness of her skin beneath his fingertips, over the faint hint of rosewater wafting from her silken hair. He savored the slight mist of her breath and the dewy moisture of her drying tears.

Roxie's nerves jumped in panic beneath the hands that still clasped her arms. Her pulse leaped out of control. Her tears dried, and she knew she should tell him to release her. But if she were honest enough to admit it, she'd have opted to have him hold her more tightly still. She wasn't ready to admit this, though, not even to herself. Especially now that that her ankle was throbbing all the way up to her knee.

"I'll drive you home," he said after what seemed like an eternity.

"You don't have to do that." At the same time that she wanted him to do it, she didn't want him to feel like she was applying undue pressure. "I can drive myself."

She might as well have saved her breath. As if she'd not raised the least objection, he put his arm around her waist and half-lifted her. Deciding might was right, she leaned against him and put her arm as far around his shoulders as she could. Together, they hobbled unsteadily outside.

Roxie's heart pounded more fiercely with each uneven step. The pulsing in her blood surpassed that of her injured ankle. In fact, she was hardly aware of her ankle. She was hardly aware of anything beyond the arm around her waist, the hand resting on her hip, the solid musculature of the man beside her. He was all firm sinews and tanned skin, and she luxuriated in his physical strength. Slanting more closely against his side, she told herself she was doing so only because she'd been knocked dizzy.

Luke's senses filled to overflowing. Her profile dominated his vision. Her hushed breathing resounded in his ears. He inhaled the sweet scent of her rosewater and absorbed her soft warmth as she pressed against his side. Each sensation tantalized him, teasing his imagination, tempting him almost beyond endurance. By the time they reached her car, he was aching with desire.

He helped her into the passenger seat with something akin to relief and then walked slowly around to the front of her old black car, grateful that he had something to focus on besides the painful excitement of wanting her.

She stuck her head out her open window and said, "I'll set the hand brake so it doesn't lurch forward when you turn the crank."

He nodded and, leaning over, jerked the crank around. A molten ball of sun bounced heat waves off the parking lot and coated his back with a damp heat. He felt burned all the way through.

He slipped behind the steering wheel but sat immobile, staring at the dashboard and wondering if he even remembered how to drive. They said it was like riding a bike, that you never forgot, but the sinking feeling in his stomach made him think they didn't know what they were talking about.

She tapped his arm and he started. "The key," she said, pointing to the coil box. "You have to turn the key."

He did, and the motor purred, but he still didn't press his foot down on the gas pedal.

"Is anything wrong?" she asked.

He glanced her way. She appeared puzzled, a bit wary even. He could take anything but having her fear him. "Not really," he answered, trying to sound casual. "It's just that I haven't driven since I"—he stopped before he could say "stole that car" and changed it to a more appropriate—"I haven't driven in a long time."

She looked down at her lap, where her hands were locked together atop her purse, and then back up at him. "Luke, you really don't have to—"

"Don't worry, Roxie, I'll get you home in one piece." Hoping he could make good on his word, he released the brake, moved the gear shift lever and stepped on the pedal to feed gas to the engine.

The car rolled forward out of the parking lot and onto the recently-paved highway.

Stewart's Warehouse sat at the farthest edge of town, almost a mile from where Route 40 met the asphalt road where they needed to turn. The yellow sun hovered in the western sky, promising the summer would continue on its scorching path, and the air was heavy with heat and humidity. The damp, almost musty smell of the Little Blue River wafted in one open window and out the other as they rumbled across the bridge. When they turned right and started up the hill toward town, a big brown dog ran out at the car and chased it a ways before sighting a cat in a ditch and taking off after it.

On the outskirts of town, Roxie gave Luke directions to her house and then lapsed into silence. She looked out the window, trying to ignore the strength of his hands as they steered the wheel, the length of his fingers as they gripped the throttle lever, the bunching of his thigh muscles under his jeans as he worked the clutch. The images seemed to have imprinted themselves over the passing landscape, however, so she dropped her head back against the seat and let her eyes sink shut.

For his part, Luke was just grateful that she didn't seem to expect him to make small talk. Under the circumstances, he wouldn't have known what to say to her anyway. But even without words, even with the unfamiliar driving to distract him, he remained tensely conscious of her. Each time she shifted, even slightly, his body heated in response.

Seven years without a woman. It was little wonder that her mere proximity roused him so readily. Yet he was certain that if he'd spent the last seven years in a sheik's harem instead of the hoosegow, he'd still react as strongly to Roxie. She was a uniquely beautiful person.

He glanced at her again. Framed by breeze-tossed tumbles of honey-colored hair, her profile had a classic old-world aura. To him she looked utterly feminine and unbearably desirable. He riveted his gaze to the road so intently that he almost didn't notice when, halfway up the hill, they encountered a car coming down. The passing motorist raised his hand to wave and then, upon seeing who was driving her car, dropped both his hand and his jaw.

No longer tucked within the unsettling circle of his arm, Roxie regained enough of her senses to wonder what on earth had come over her. What would her parents say when she rode up with Luke Bauer? She might as well come home with that notorious criminal, Machine Gun Kelly! Why hadn't she sensibly phoned them when he first suggested it?

Why hadn't she, indeed? She opened her eyes and straightened in her seat, looking out the window at the water tower on which the town's name was painted. Such questions were better left unanswered.

The wheels bumped over the road with agonizing slowness. She was certain she could have limped home more quickly. Surely this drive had never before taken so long, nor had her car ever been driven so carefully. She couldn't believe they could be going at a normal speed and still be taking so long to get home. Each minute confined with him, locked in this weighty silence with her recriminating questions, seemed neverending.

And then she saw the sign to her street and felt she barely had any time left with him at all. She rushed into speech, not even realizing that she'd been planning her apology all along. "Luke, I'm sorry about all this, about disrupting your evening, and—"

"You didn't disrupt anything, Roxie," he told her truthfully. "Not this or any other evening."

"I shouldn't have bothered you," she continued as if he hadn't spoken. "I really do thank you for going out of your way like this for me."

He couldn't believe his ears. Didn't she realize that he'd have done far more for her, carried her home on his back if necessary? He'd never felt such concern for anyone in his life as he had when he'd seen her face whiten with pain, and now she was actually apologizing to him. It affected him in a myriad of ways, ways he couldn't begin to describe.

"Don't worry about it," he said in an offhand fashion that had nothing to do with what he was feeling.

"Here." She pointed to a two-story Craftsman-style house that was set back from the street. "This is it."

Luke parked in the private driveway behind a big black

Packard. He let his hands slide from the wheel and heaved a sigh of relief at the realization that he'd made it without incident. When he got out of the car and cut around to help Roxie out, he could see the leafy oak trees standing on either side of the meticulously-manicured lawn. A Midwest cottage garden of more plants than he could name filled the space between the front walk and the foundation of the house, while fat pots of colorful blooms marched up the steps leading to the entry porch.

Looking around, he recognized this as one of the neighborhoods he used to cut through on his way to and from school. In his mind's eye he could see the lonely little boy standing on the sidewalk looking at the beautiful houses located here. Houses where laughter rang and voices sang. Houses where mothers made hot breakfasts for their children on cold mornings and fathers returned from work of an evening full of the day's news instead of booze.

Homes, he realized now as lights began winking on behind curtained windows, casting out their welcoming yellow glow as the tall old trees threw their shadows across the street and the yards that bordered it. These weren't houses; they were homes. And recognizing that made him realize that he'd never had a home himself.

The lights were on in Roxie's house, too, he noticed, but he wasn't at all sure what kind of welcome he was going to receive. No matter. He'd brought her this far. He'd take her the rest of the way.

Roxie's heartbeat accelerated as she again accepted his support. With his arm wrapped supportively around her, she staggered toward the front steps. Even the distraction of Luke's touch couldn't suppress her discomfort. The pain was worse now, shooting through her with each tiny jolt.

Luke took one look at her wan face and white-rimmed lips

and didn't hesitate. He swung her up in his arms and lithely mounted the steps.

Roxie didn't protest. She didn't want to. She felt secure, comforted, protected. Her only regret was that there were so few steps.

Once Luke reached the porch, she opened the heavy wood door and he shouldered through, into an oak-floored foyer that was almost bigger than his room in the boardinghouse.

The whirling blades of the ceiling fan provided a cool respite from the heat. He toed the front door closed as the grandfather clock in the corner of the entryway chimed the time. Six-fifteen. Which meant they were either a little early or a little late for dinner.

"Roxie? Is that you?" called her unseen mother. "Hurry up, we've just sat down."

"Which way?" Luke asked, whispering.

Pointing left, Roxie whispered back, "They're in the dining room."

As he strode into the room with her firmly clasped in his arms, there was an absolutely still moment in which shock rippled down the table, from her mother at one end to her brother Frederick and his wife Nora sitting next to each other in the middle to her father at the other end.

The second wave of reaction was more varied, including her parents' clearly visible concern, her sister-in-law's obvious curiosity, and her brother's equally obvious antagonism. Roxie watched their changing expressions and felt her pleasure in Luke's arms fade. She wiggled within his grasp, indicating she wanted to be set down, but he simply tightened his hold.

"Roxie twisted her ankle," he announced to one and all. "It looks like it could be a bad sprain."

Hearing the trace of aggression in his voice, she looked at him in sharp surprise. He'd never used that tone in her presence, not even tonight when he'd been so determined to bring her home. But the surprise she felt was nothing compared to her family's. She could see it darkening the chandelier-lit room and decided the moment called for a quick explanation.

"It was just a silly accident," she said. "I fell in the warehouse, and if Luke hadn't been there to drive me home, I don't know what I would have done. My ankle is already three times its normal size."

Her mother rose with a series of brisk instructions. "Nora, get some towels from the upstairs bathroom. Frederick, bring up that small soaking tub from the basement. William, the footstool is in my sewing room."

Chairs rasped, voices clashed, steps rapped over hardwood as the rest of the family jumped obediently to do her bidding. Mary briefly inspected Roxie's ankle and told her to take her stocking and shoe off. Then she darted into the kitchen to get some ice and run some cold water.

Luke felt like he'd walked into the eye of a tornado.

Returning with the footstool, William recognized the look on his face and laughed, startling him. "You may have noticed that Mary is a regular whirlwind of efficiency. Even after thirty-five years together," the older man added, "I still find the wind knocked out of me when she's like this."

"Yes, sir," Luke said, feeling at a real loss. He'd expected hostility from William, or demands to unhand his daughter—at the very best a reserved thanks. He would have known how to handle any of those, but this left him dumfounded. He watched warily as the gray-haired man moved to the side of the table, pulled out a chair and set the footstool in front of it. Even in his open-collared white shirt and comfortable blue sweater, he conveyed an air of authority.

"Unless you're of a mind to hold on to my daughter forever," he said dryly, "I'd suggest you put her down here."

"Yes, sir," he repeated. He'd rather have held on to her, but he set Roxie on the chair and then backed into a shadowed corner.

Her father ruffled her hair with a gentle hand before he bent to remove her peep-toed pump, his body shielding her as she raised her skirt above her knee to release her stocking from the garter that kept it up and roll it down her leg. She began relating the accident in amusing detail and the two laughed together. The loving intimacy made Luke feel like an intruder. Beginning to wish he could simply vanish into thin air, he started edging his way out of the room.

Mary swept in from the kitchen, followed by a stony-faced Frederick, and within minutes Roxie's bare foot was soaking in a small round tub of ice water. She let out a little yelp of distress at the frigidity, and her brother claimed she deserved it for being so reckless. Nora returned with the towel as well as a plump pillow for Roxie to rest her foot on after she'd soaked it. Nora had hardly set the two items on the sideboard when Mary sent her to fetch another place setting for Luke.

Hearing this, he stopped before he could make good his escape. He couldn't possibly intrude any further. Already, he'd stayed too long. He didn't belong in this beautiful home, at that family table, and he knew better than to wish he did.

"That's not necessary, Mrs. Mitchell," he said flatly.

"But of course you're staying to dine, Mr. Bauer."

"I don't think I—"

"Have you eaten?"

"No, ma'am."

"Then you'll eat with us," she declared in a tone that brooked no argument. "It's the least we can do to repay you for your kindness to Roxie."

"Oh, I was glad—"

"Sit down, please."

A slender woman with her salt-and-pepper hair done in a series of close waves around her pretty, unlined face, Mary Mitchell looked a lot like her daughter. But she had an inexorable way of speaking that Luke didn't think Roxie would ever cultivate. Perhaps being the mother of four and grandmother of three—soon to be four—had made it necessary for her to sound as if she meant whatever she said. But just the same, he couldn't quite accept that she really meant for him to sit at her table and share her food. After all, he was a Bauer.

William cleared his throat. "The house rule is that Mary is never wrong at dinnertime. So I suggest you sit yourself down while you're still able to do so."

Roxie patted the seat of the chair beside her. "Please, Luke, sit here."

And still he just stood there, half in and half out of the dining room, wanting very much to stay but believing strongly that he shouldn't.

Nora came in from the kitchen, her hands filled with a plate, silverware and a napkin, which she arranged on the embroidered tablecloth.

Luke glanced at Roxie's brother. Frederick hadn't spoken, but he didn't need to. His narrowed eyes and the reproachful set of his lips beneath a thin mustache made it perfectly apparent that he'd prefer having the influenza in for dinner.

"Our meal is getting cold," Mary pointed out.

He gave in. He'd wanted to, anyway, but now he could do so in good conscience. The brother could go hang. He sat down and bowed his head while William intoned grace. This is the way it is in real families, he thought. The way it might have been in his family if his mother hadn't run off, if his father hadn't been a drunk, if he could have lived with his grandfather. If, if, if.

A collective "amen" cut off his thoughts and told him it was time to eat.

Honey fried chicken, new potatoes creamed with freshly-shelled peas, and thick slices of red, ripe tomatoes picked from the backyard garden attracted his attention. He realized he was famished and dug in with relish.

For a few minutes the sound of a meal in progress dominated the room, but then the Mitchells got down to their nightly discussions. They spoke of general things—the ongoing drought, the withering crops, the depressed economy. And they spoke of specific things—the cute and clever antics of Bill and Marlene's children, John's decision to plant soybeans to replenish the soil and Lee's pregnancy, Frederick and Nora's upcoming trip to Clay Center, Kansas, to visit her parents and siblings.

Luke sat quietly, enwrapped in the loving comfort of their conversation. Emotions began churning within him, tender emotions he'd thought long dead, emotions that somehow centered on Roxie. He permitted himself a covert look at her. She unexpectedly looked his way. The clear blue of her gaze melted into the gray yearning of his. A moment passed, then another.

Their silent exchange didn't go unnoticed. Luke suddenly became aware of the growing silence that surrounded them and glanced about the table. The questioning looks he saw had him averting his eyes to his empty plate.

"I think my foot has gone numb," Roxie told her mother. "I can't feel a thing, not even the water."

"Just keep that foot where it is," Mary ordered. "After dessert we'll wrap it, and then you'll elevate it a while."

Roxie pretended to pout, and it was all Luke could do not to laugh.

A still-curious Nora poured coffee while Mary fetched cake from the kitchen.

"So what happened?" Nora asked as she resumed her seat.

"I knocked Roxie down," Luke admitted.

"Actually, I ran into him," she clarified. "I'd stayed late to finish typing up one last order and was hurrying to get out of there. I deserve a sprained ankle for not looking where I was going."

"How will you get to work tomorrow?" Nora passed on dessert, patting her flat stomach to indicate she was too full from dinner, and then pointed out the obvious. "You can't drive yourself. You wouldn't have gotten home tonight if Luke hadn't driven you."

"Speaking of that," Frederick intervened, and Luke tensed. He knew the note of trouble when he heard it. He knew the look, too, and Frederick definitely wore it. Now Frederick leaned back in his chair, narrowly scrutinizing Luke, as if he'd been waiting for his chance and was about to seize it. "Speaking of that," he repeated, "it's occurred to me that I haven't seen you driving around town before. At least, not since you got back from prison."

Hot color flooded into her cheeks as Roxie thought fleetingly of giving Frederick a swift under-the-table kick, sprained ankle and all.

"That's probably because I don't own a car," Luke said in a measured tone.

"As I recall," Frederick returned pointedly, "you stole a car before you robbed that gasoline station."

"That's right," Luke clipped out.

An uncomfortable hush settled over the table. William and Mary exchanged a look. Ignoring her contentious husband, Nora patted her finger-waved hair. Roxie sat as still as a stone, not stirring by so much as a breath.

Well, all dreams come to an end, Luke thought. He'd felt all night as if he'd been in a dream, the sort of fantasy he hadn't allowed himself to indulge in since he was a child. Realizing he'd overstayed his welcome, he started to push back his chair and excuse himself from the table.

"More cake?" Mary asked him, reaching for the glass dessert plate.

Luke paused, looking from what remained of the chocolate-iced Scotch cake to her in puzzled surprise. She pushed the plate toward him. He slowly shook his head. "No, thank you."

"I'll leave it in case you change your mind." She stood. "Nora, will you help me clear the table?"

Normally the men would have retired to the oak-paneled library for an after-dinner smoke while the women finished up in the kitchen. But in deference to Roxie's injury they remained seated at the dining room table. After retrieving a clean crystal ashtray from the top drawer of the sideboard, William set it on the table, pulled a pack of cigarettes from the pocket of his sweater and tapped one out.

"Cigarette?" William offered the pack to Luke.

Luke shook his head and said wryly, "That's probably the only vice I haven't indulged in."

William laughed. "Ah, well, you're smart not to. I've had the habit since high school and have never been able to get rid of it."

"I've heard it's a hard one to shake."

"Tell me, Luke," William said then, "what are your plans now that you're home?"

The question caught Luke off-guard. His gaze shot to the older man, whose face wrinkled in a kindly way. Still, he didn't lower his guard. "Plans?"

"Do you plan to learn a trade?" he prompted. "Or maybe go to college?"

"Outside of doing the best job I can at the warehouse, I really haven't made any plans," Luke admitted.

"You probably need some time to figure things out."

"One thing I would like to do is to go by my grandfather's old place someday soon and see what's become of it."

William got an odd look on his face, but before he could respond Frederick took center stage. He stood, said "Excuse me" in a brusque tone of voice that declared he didn't care whether they excused him or not, and stamped from the room. His exit seemed to go unnoticed by his father and sister but not by Luke. He stared at the vacated chair, almost wishing Frederick hadn't gone. He knew how to deal with that type of animosity. It was the others' kindness that unsettled him.

A hand touched his knee. He cast a startled eye toward Roxie. She smiled that soft, sweet smile that made his heart hitch.

"Don't worry about Frederick," she said softly. "He'll get over it."

He wasn't worried about Frederick, not in the least. It was this upheaval within himself that had him worried. What he said was, "Maybe it's time I got on my way."

But he didn't go. He stayed to carry Roxie into the parlor, lowering her gently into an overstuffed club chair so Mary could dry and wrap her daughter's ankle and prop it on the footstool William brought in. He stayed even after Frederick and Nora made a hasty and, on his part at least, somewhat huffy exit. He stayed to listen to William's dry observations on both the local and national political scene. Most of all, he stayed to pretend, for a short while longer, he was a part of it, to imagine he belonged.

It passed all too quickly. Though he tried to hold it back, the time spun away. It seemed a matter of mere seconds before William rose, stretched and offered to drive him home.

Reluctantly Luke came to his feet. "Thank you, Mr. Mitchell, but I can walk."

"Are you sure?"

"I just live across the railroad tracks." The irony of his being right back where he'd started from didn't escape Luke.

"I'm on the welcoming committee at church," Mary said then. "Perhaps you'd like to attend services next Sunday."

"Now, Mary—" William started to intervene.

"Or any Sunday of your choosing," she quickly amended.

Luke bit his tongue before he could tell her that the roof and the walls of the church would probably cave in if he showed up. Instead he just nodded in a noncommittal manner and replied with stiff formality, "Thank you, Mrs. Mitchell. I don't know when I've had such a delicious meal, nor such a pleasant evening."

He wasn't exactly being truthful. He did know. He'd never had food that tasted so good. He'd never had an evening so imbued with a welcoming warmth.

"Nonsense," Mary said in her brisk way. "It's we who thank you—for bringing Roxie home."

"He should have let me limp home," Roxie put in. "But he's too much of a gentleman."

Their eyes met, and Luke felt a surge of desire unlike anything he'd ever known. The heat blazed from his loins to the center of his being, where he lived and breathed and didn't have to think. Some gentleman, he thought with self-derision, and harshly reminded himself that such desires could never be fulfilled.

Suddenly anxious to be leaving, he bid her and her parents a restrained good-night and strode out.

# CHAPTER 6

The number of people living under her roof might have grown smaller, but Mary Mitchell still believed in big breakfasts.

This morning was no exception. Her kitchen table, a round oak affair sitting in the middle of the cheery apple green room and covered with a clean oilcloth, held platters of buckwheat pancakes, bacon fried to a perfect crisp, fluffy scrambled eggs, and warmed-over biscuits. A small jar of homemade strawberry jam and a glass pitcher of syrup topped off the array.

After filling everyone's coffee cup, she hung her apron on a wall hook near the stove, took her chair and bowed her head for the blessing. Then, smiling at her husband, daughter and oldest son, she said as she did every morning, "Well, are you going to let it all get cold?"

As if on cue, hands shot out to pass plates around the table while chattering voices harmonized with clashing silverware.

Only Roxie remained silent. She'd awakened in a listless mood, her apathy spawned by the melancholy she'd taken to bed with her the night before. It had been so unexpected, that abrupt withdrawal of Luke's as he'd said good night, that her joy in the evening had instantly crumbled.

Up to then she'd felt a blossoming happiness. Her heart had swelled with love for her parents, for their unequivocal acceptance of Luke. She had not even known how very much it meant to her until Frederick had made it abundantly clear that he, for one, did not accept Luke. But even that hadn't dampened her spirits. It had taken Luke to do that. One long look at her and he'd withdrawn. She'd seen it in his eyes, she'd heard it in his voice, and she'd ached with the grieving pain of loss.

Her reaction stunned her, then depressed her. She didn't understand her sense of loss, but she did understand that she didn't want to feel such things—not on his account, not on any man's account. One time through that particular emotional wringer had been more than enough for her.

It hadn't improved her mood any to see that her oldest brother Bill had dropped in this morning. He came for breakfast once or twice a week, generally on the way to his insurance office, so it wasn't all that unusual to see him sitting at the table. What was unusual was the way he kept glancing at her out of the corner of his eye as he piled eggs, bacon, and biscuits on his plate. It made her suspect there was an ulterior motive behind this morning's visit.

She idly shifted a portion of eggs from one side of her plate to the other, not really interested in food. It took a good minute for her to realize that her mother was speaking to her. When she finally did, she sat up straight and put on an attentive face. "I'm sorry, Mother, what did you say?"

"I asked how your ankle is this morning." Mary gave her one of those sharp looks she had honed to perfection over the years. Without waiting for an answer to her first question, she posed a second. "Do you think you should stop by Dr. Griffin's office and have an x-ray made?"

"No, I'm sure nothing's broken," Roxie reassured her. "It's not even that much of a sprain, just a twist really."

"Still, you'll probably need to be driven to work today."

"Oh, I think I can drive myself."

"You probably could last night," her brother muttered around a mouthful of eggs.

Roxie set her fork down and stared across the table at him. This was it, she realized, the real reason he'd stopped by. She knew the town was buzzing with gossip about her hiring Luke. Everywhere she went, be it the general store, the bank or even the movie house, she saw people clustering together when she passed by. She could only imagine what they would all say if they knew that Luke had driven her home and carried her into the house.

She couldn't confront each and every rumormonger, of course, but maybe she could put a stop to her brother's blathering. Toward that end, she strove to ask in a calm voice, "What, exactly, did you mean by that?"

Bill expertly speared a pancake from the platter centered on the table and plopped it onto his plate before replying. He'd gained weight since becoming a husband and father, and it didn't sit particularly well on him. His cheeks had plumped out, his once sharply-defined jaw line had softened some, and he had developed a small paunch that the jacket of his suit couldn't disguise.

"I'm just wondering how bad your ankle was in the first place," he said. "Did you really need someone to drive you home and carry you into the house? Or were you using one of the oldest female tricks in the book?"

"You've spoken to Frederick," she concluded, her voice turning edgy.

"He and Nora stopped by on their way home from here last night," he acknowledged as he slathered butter on his pancake.

Roxie's mouth twitched once before she controlled it. "Well, even if I had been using such a trick—which my swollen ankle more than proved I was not—what concern is it of yours?"

"You just happen to be my sister." Bill picked up the syrup pitcher and poured, drowning his pancake in the sweet, sticky liquid. "And I'm very naturally concerned when I hear my sister has come home in the arms of a known criminal."

"That's what he was," she clipped out, "not what he is."

"Come on, Roxie," he said in a condescending tone, "how naïve can you get? He is what he is, what he always has been."

"Don't you believe in giving someone a chance?" She lifted a hand almost in a pleading gesture, then let it fall. "Don't you think people can change?"

Bill snorted in disgust. "I think Clyde Barrow and Bonnie Parker can change into model citizens if they so choose, but I sincerely doubt that's going to happen."

"Oh, for the love of—" Roxie swept up her fork and stabbed at a crispy piece of bacon, breaking it in half, then dropped the utensil back onto her plate with a clatter. "All he did was bring me home!"

"Probably to see what Mother and Dad have that's worth taking," he shot back.

A heated flush swept up her neck to her cheeks. She thought of a dozen retorts but bit them back. It would be futile to go on arguing. He was too certain he was right to be swayed by anything she said. Perhaps, given time, he'd reassess his judgment of Luke. Or perhaps not.

"What I can't believe," Bill said, glancing irately from their mother to their father, "is that you two are so complacent about this. Do you *want* Roxie to get involved with a convict?"

The sudden silence in the kitchen was broken only by the ticking of the wall clock. Everyone sat immobile, paralyzed by the grip of tension. For a long moment, Roxie stared down at her plate, waiting for one of her parents to respond to her brother's question.

"What we want, son," their father finally and firmly stated, "is to enjoy our breakfast in peace."

An awkward shuffling of feet and shifting on chairs preceded the mute resumption of the meal. Bill finished first. Shoving his empty plate away, he kissed his mother on the cheek, nodded at his father and, ignoring the sister he claimed to be so concerned about, left the house.

That suited Roxie just fine. She ate nothing more, simply continued pushing the food around. When her father excused himself, she picked up his plate and utensils along with her own and limped across the kitchen with them in hand. After setting the dishes in the sink, she began packing her lunch. She was angrily spreading butter on bread to accompany the chicken leg she'd selected from last night's leftovers when Mary came up beside her.

"Do you think the stork made a mistake?"

Roxie looked askance at her mother. "What?"

"Do you think perhaps it brought me the wrong child?" Mary tied on her ruffle-edged apron and began scraping plates and running a hot-water suds to wash them in. "Bill can be so bullheaded on occasion. He simply can't be mine. It must have been the stork's error."

"I don't feel like being humored, Mother."

"No? What do you feel like?"

Roxie slapped her sandwich together and cut it in half. "I feel like knocking some sense into Bill."

"Now, isn't that odd?" her mother mused. "I've the distinct impression that he feels precisely like doing the same to you."

The knife clattered to the floor. Roxie blew out an irritated breath as she picked it up, put it in the sink and got a clean one out of the silverware drawer. When she reached over to cut herself a piece of leftover Scotch cake, Mary clasped her hand, stilling the restless agitation.

"For what it's worth, Roxie," she said softly, "I don't think you need some sense knocked into you. But I do think you should take care."

She met her mother's unfaltering gaze. Tolerance shone in

Mary's hazel eyes, but concern dimmed their normal brightness. Willfully getting a grip on her temper, Roxie took a deep breath.

"You needn't worry," she said, seeking to soothe her mother's fears. "Bill's blown this totally out of proportion, that's all."

"I'll always worry about my children—"

"That's what mothers are for," Roxie finished for her. A smile played over her mouth. She'd heard that one so many times it was probably engraved in her heart. "Okay, Mother, worry all you want. Who am I to stop you? But believe me, there's no need to waste your time and energy."

Mary wagged a teasing finger at her. "It's my time and my energy; I'll waste it if I wish." Then she turned back toward the table to finish clearing it, saying as she did, "Why don't you take him that last piece of cake to eat with his chicken and bread-and-butter sandwich?"

Roxie stared blankly at her mother's back for a few shocked seconds. Then she closed her dropped jaw and, laughing, reached for the cake plate and two more slices of bread.

Setting the cloth bag that held their lunches on the tabletop, Roxie pulled out two wrapped pieces of chicken, two bread-and-butter sandwiches and two slices of cake. Then she sat down in her chair and waited. She knew Luke's routine almost better than he did. He would go to the icebox to get a sandwich and then, carrying his glass jug of water, he would head outside. But not today. Not if she could help it. Where, after all, was it written that they couldn't be friends?

The murmuring that drifted through the lunchroom would have told her he'd arrived even if the jangling of her nerves had not. Standing, she put on a wide, welcoming smile. The low hum around her deepened.

Roxie paid no mind to it. Her attention was riveted on Luke.

He eclipsed everything and everyone else. He always had. In the old days, if she'd thought about it at all, she would have assumed it was due to his cocky stride, his bold stance, his smug expression. He'd had a way of looking as if he owned whatever piece of property he happened to be standing on. He didn't look cocky right now, yet his effect was precisely the same.

Just inside the doorway, his steps slowed as if he sensed something was different. He swept a hand through glossy black hair that had grown some but was as unruly as ever and looked around him. Roxie's mouth went dry and her tummy tightened when he glanced her way. He stopped dead as their gazes locked. Still smiling, she crooked her index finger and beckoned him over.

Luke wavered briefly and then slowly approached the table. How often had he fantasized about her warm smile? How painfully had he yearned for it? He tried to tell himself that she was generous with her smiles, that she smiled at everyone, that she had no way of knowing what it meant to him. But a bolt of excitement shot through him nonetheless.

A dozen clever things to say flew through Roxie's mind as he neared the table. But she'd also had time to remember all the occasions that he'd rebuffed her over the past few weeks and so she remained silent. Would he reject her again? Had last night changed anything? Was she a fool to believe they really could be friends?

"Hello," she managed at last.

He nodded a greeting and looked down. "How's the ankle?"

She stuck out her leg and wiggled her foot. The cloth wrap her mother had applied the night before was barely visible beneath the white anklet she wore with her brown lace-up oxfords today. "Much better, thank you."

"Were you able to drive yourself to work?"

"I was, and it didn't bother me a bit."

"Swell," he said, and then, feeling everyone's eyes on them, repeated himself. "Swell."

It was new to Luke, this sharing of simple memories and good-natured remarks. But a rising tension pierced his pleasure. He glanced around. A clearly avid curiosity gripped the lunchroom. As much as he regretted it, he knew he had to put an end to this sweet interlude. But still he lingered.

Roxie cleared her throat. "Thank you again for taking me home last night."

"Forget it. I was happy to do it." He gave her one of those conversation-ending waves of the hand and made to move away.

"I brought lunch for you," she said quickly. She indicated the food she'd arranged on the table. "Mother even sent the last of the Scotch cake as a special treat. It doesn't keep well in this heat. The cake dries out and the chocolate icing melts and gets all gooey, and then it's just a mess to eat."

He gazed steadily at her but didn't reply.

Feeling nervous now, she yammered on. "If you don't help me out, I'm going to have to eat two lunches all by myself."

Luke continued staring at her, not really believing the entreaty he saw in her beautiful blue eyes. He longed to touch the curve of her lips, to feel the smile he was seeing, to know the reality of it. But her smile gradually faded into a puzzled frown. She tipped her head and the honey gold of her hair whisked softly against the shoulder seam of her simple blue blouse. He stared and he hungered, but not for the lunch.

"It's chicken left over from our dinner last night as well as bread-and-butter sandwiches to go with it," she prompted.

And still he just stood there staring at her.

She reached for the chicken pieces she'd set out, partially unwrapped them and passed them slowly in front of his nose, trying to tempt him. "Which piece do you prefer? A leg or a thigh? I remember you ate one of each last night."

He snapped to his senses, and not a moment too soon. A swift survey told him that everyone had heard her, that they all now realized they had eaten dinner together the night before, and that they were watching them even more keenly than ever. "Thank you," he said stiffly, "but—"

"Don't you dare try to decline my mother's chicken and cake." She knew by his stilted response just what he'd seen in that quick appraisal, and all her indignant hackles were raised. She drew herself up ramrod straight, sounding amazingly like Mary at her maternal best. "Now, if you'd be so kind as to get me a cup of coffee with no sugar but lots of milk . . ."

Without waiting to see if he accepted her imperative invitation, Roxie unwrapped the rest of their lunch. By the time she smoothed out the waxed paper that held their food and divided the luncheon napkins and forks that she'd brought from home, it was patently obvious that she had planned this lunch down to the last detail. Throughout the room the buzz of speculation took on the drone of certainty.

Luke thought she'd gone stark, staring mad. He quietly said as much when he returned with her coffee and his full water jug. She answered by pointing to the wooden chair across from hers.

"Don't you care that they're all talking about you?" he demanded almost angrily.

"No," she said with a dismissive shake of her head before asking him again, "Which piece—the leg or the thigh?"

"The thigh." He knew when to give in, especially when he wanted to anyway. If she didn't care what they thought, he certainly wasn't going to try to convince her otherwise. He sat down, picked up his chicken and took a bite.

"It's as good cold as it was hot," she said.

"Cold or hot, it's delicious," he answered truthfully.

"Mother drenches the chicken pieces in honey before she

flours and fries them."

"Where does she get the honey?"

"She used to buy it from your grandfather—I remember how good his honey tasted on her warm biscuits—but I don't know where she buys it now."

"Regardless, she's a wonderful cook."

"She certainly is," Roxie agreed.

Luke chewed and swallowed. "What about you?"

"Me?"

"Can you cook?"

She made a so-so gesture with her hand. "I make really good cookies, if that counts for anything."

That got his attention. "What kind of cookies?"

"Molasses is my specialty."

"They're my favorite."

"Well, then, you can sample them on Saturday."

He paused with his bread-and-butter sandwich halfway to his mouth. "You're making molasses cookies on Saturday?"

"Actually, I'm making them on Friday night, in the church basement, and then selling them on Saturday. Or rather, the Ladies Aide is selling them." She dabbed at her mouth with her napkin. "It's how we raise money for the charities we sponsor."

"What charities are those?"

"Well, Saturday's proceeds will go to buy books for the town library." She put down her napkin and picked up her sandwich. "Then next month's will go to help buy whatever the orphan's home needs."

He mulled that over as he chewed and swallowed. "And just where will you be selling your cookies?"

"Dad lets us set up a table in the lobby of the bank."

"I promised to paint my landlady's porch, but I'll try to stop by."

"The bank closes at noon on Saturday," she reminded him.

He nodded. "I should be finished by then."

For several minutes they ate in silence, but she was keenly aware of him watching her. When he finished his chicken, she pointed to the piece of cake she'd set in front of him. "If you don't eat every bite of that, you'll receive one of my mother's infamous tongue-lashings."

"Spare me that," he said in mock horror. "I've known wardens who could take lessons from your mother."

She sputtered, choking back her laughter. "You shouldn't joke about a girl's mother."

He found himself smiling again. It was a remarkably easy thing to do around her. He swigged some water, then drawled, "I don't think I'd call your mother a joke. Fact is, I happen to admire her a great deal."

It was on the tip of her tongue to say something ridiculous like, *You should smile more often,* but she sensibly swallowed the frivolous comment and said breezily, "Oh, you're right. My mother is no joke. Neither is my father, for that matter." His smile wavered and then faded. He looked down at what remained of his lunch, then up at her. "Last night," he said slowly, "meeting your parents . . . I enjoyed myself very much." He'd never be able to express how much.

"I'm glad, Luke, really glad. We enjoyed having you." Roxie looked at him expectantly. "Maybe you could come again some-time."

"But not too soon," he said without thinking. He saw her stiffen and sprang into an explanation. "I didn't mean that the way it sounded."

She sat back in her chair. "Oh?"

He shrugged. "I should have said I'm just not used to being social yet."

Her expression went blank.

"People don't realize how noisy prison is," he explained.

"There's non-stop racket, what with doors slamming, sirens blaring, inmates yelling and fighting. Even the guards add to it. They holler orders and drag their batons across the metal bars. And when the prisoners get too rowdy, the guards turn their radios all the way up."

She drew a breath that caused her chest to shudder. "It sounds horrible."

"It is."

She almost reached across the table to touch his hand in consolation but caught herself before she did.

He took another drink of water before he went on. "Now I live alone, and trying to talk to people, to keep up my end of a conversation, well, in all honesty, it tires me out."

Relief pumped through her at the realization that he'd simply been tired when he left last night. "I didn't realize."

"How could you?" he said, struggling to keep from sounding bitter. "You've never known an ex-con, much less had one drive you home."

She looked away, her heart curling up into a ball of sadness at his bleak tone. Then, remembering Frederick's caustic remarks from the night before, she faced him squarely. "What if we'd been stopped by the sheriff for some reason? What could have happened?"

Now he shifted uncomfortably. "We weren't, so why bother talking about it?"

"But if we had been, Luke, what then?" Roxie persisted. "I think I've a right to know."

He could see she wasn't going to let it go and blew out an exasperated breath. "If we had been stopped for some reason, say, because I was driving too fast or too slow, or maybe even because I wasn't holding my mouth right enough to suit him, the sheriff would likely have found some reason to haul me in and throw the book at me."

Swallowing a sip of coffee, she spoke with conviction. "You shouldn't have taken the chance. Not on my account."

Luke thought his heart would simply burst. Except for his grandfather, he couldn't remember anyone else ever caring about what he did or what might happen to him as a result. Forcing an easygoing note into his voice now, he said, "You're right. Next time you hurt your ankle, I'll leave you to suffer. Even if it's broken, I won't come near you."

She shook her hair back and looked at him with feigned exasperation. "I wasn't talking about me. Just my car."

"Afraid I'll steal it, huh?" he teased.

Roxie couldn't help herself, she erupted into laughter. As it waned, she pressed her lips together and said primly, "There is that to worry about."

Luke laughed, too. Then he picked up his fork and cut himself a bite of cake. While he was at it, he changed the subject. "How did you come to work here, anyway?"

"I needed a job when I came back from St. Louis," she said without thinking her answer through.

"You lived in St. Louis?" He was truly surprised. There was so much about her that he didn't know, that he had no right to know.

She slid her gaze away from his. "After I graduated from college, I worked for a dress manufacturing company there."

The small evasion told him a great deal. Someone had hurt her, badly, and even though he didn't know who, he hated the person who'd caused her hurt. But it was clear she didn't want to talk about it. And given his own history, he was the last person on earth to probe into another's painful memories.

Foregoing any questions about her previous job, he washed the last of his cake down with a drink of water. "I heard you'd gone away to school but figured you wanted to become a nurse or a teacher."

Roxie felt her cheeks flush. It was what he didn't say, what he didn't ask, that spurred her to explain. "Actually, I studied accounting."

"So you didn't like accounting."

The statement held a question, one Roxie longed more than anything to ignore. But she couldn't. He'd opened up to her questioning a few weeks ago. Now it was her turn to keep the slender thread of communication between them from snapping.

"No, I liked accounting well enough." Seeing he'd finished his slice of cake, she pushed hers toward him and was pleased when he dug into it. "I do quite a bit of it here and now, in fact. It was . . . St. Louis . . . that didn't agree with me."

Luke had learned to spot a lie. In prison his life had sometimes depended on it. But in a world without a moment of privacy he'd also learned to respect the sanctum of another's privacy.

He gave her an out. "You must have missed your family, gotten homesick."

A grateful smile lit her face, adding a dewy glow to her natural beauty. "I did. I missed them terribly. But to tell you the truth, they were the main reason I left in the first place."

He found it hard to believe her. Given a family like hers, given the love and the warmth, the caring and the sharing, he'd have stayed put for eternity. They said you couldn't miss what you'd never had, but they didn't know what they were talking about. He'd never had the loving support of a family like the Mitchells, and he'd missed it like hell.

Watching the skepticism cross his face, she laughed softly. "I didn't mean to imply that I didn't love them or that I wasn't happy at home."

He tilted his head. "Then what did you mean, Roxie?"

The husky way he breathed her name prompted her to reveal more than she'd intended. "You remember how you told me that all you'd ever wanted was out?"

He nodded.

"Well, I wanted out too. I needed to be on my own, to be alone for a while, to see and do things I couldn't see and do if I stayed here." She dropped her voice so low he could barely hear her. "I needed to find something or to do something that made me feel special."

He thought everything about her was special.

Roxie sighed, knowing she wasn't explaining herself very well. "What I'm trying to say is, I needed to be a person in my own right, to be someone besides my parents' only daughter or my brothers' little sister or even"—she held her hands out, palms up—"the next girl in my group of friends to get married. I needed to feel like I wasn't always lost in the crowd."

Luke couldn't imagine losing her in a crowd of thousands.

Roxie suddenly realized how silly this all must sound to him and shook her head in chagrin. "I'm sorry, Luke. I didn't mean to go on like that. You must think me a self-indulgent fool."

"No, Roxie," he said softly. "I think you're a caring and generous person who needn't ever feel less than anyone else."

Looking down, she refolded the waxed paper in which their sandwiches had been wrapped and put it and their forks back in her lunch bag for another day, leaving their napkins on the table for the time being. She couldn't meet his gaze for fear she'd blurt out the awful truth. He wouldn't think so highly of her then, and she couldn't bear the thought.

As she closed the bag for the time being, she said, "When I was in high school I developed what my mother called a rebellious streak."

He arched a skeptical brow.

She gave him a hear-me-out look. "I remember one year Dad got involved in the election for mayor, and he and Mother and my brothers practically lived at the candidate's headquarters, making signs, handing out pamphlets, running errands. But I went to work for the rival candidate." A self-deprecating smile curved her lips. "We won, too. But I didn't really care about the election. I was just being rebellious."

Luke studied her for a long moment, trying to think of something to say that she wouldn't take the wrong way. Rebellious. He could tell her a thing or two about being rebellious, none of it as tame as what she'd just related.

"I'm shocked," he said instead, angling her a solemn look that the twinkle in his eyes belied. "They should've hauled you in and thrown the book at you."

Laughing again, she balled up her used napkin and threw it at him. He caught it and, giving her another of his mesmerizing smiles, handed it back to her. They sat there a moment, co-cooned in a surprisingly comfortable silence.

"I suppose," she said at length, "it all must sound pretty stupid to you—"

"No." His face lost all vestiges of humor. "Not stupid, but blessed."

Roxie blinked in stupefaction. "What?"

"Blessed," Luke reiterated in a husky voice. He cleared his throat of the emotion churning there. Then, afraid of making a fool of himself in front of her, he pushed back his chair and lurched to his feet. "It sounded to me as if you were blessed."

And in that moment, she did indeed feel blessed.

# CHAPTER 7

"May I give you a friendly word of advice?"

Roxie looked up from the end-of-the-week ledger she had just finished preparing for Layton Stewart's perusal and saw Fesol Vernal standing on the threshold of her open office doorway.

The payroll clerk didn't wait for an invitation but rather stepped all the way inside. He closed her door behind him and unceremoniously planted his lanky form on the corner of her desk. Then, without so much as a by-your-leave, he launched into his spiel. "I hope you'll take this in the spirit in which it's given—"

"Oh, I will," Roxie interrupted dryly.

"And I assure you with all sincerity that I say this with the utmost good will," he went on, completely unaffected by her discouraging tone. "I'm concerned, not only as an employee of this company for another employee, but I'm concerned about you as a friend."

She thought about disputing the fact that they were friends but decided to hold her tongue.

"You can't know how worried I've been," he began.

Well, at least she agreed with something he said. She couldn't know. And to be perfectly honest, she didn't want to know. Clearing her throat, she tried to keep him from going any further. "Fesol—"

"How worried we've all been," he continued doggedly. "Now

I've taken it upon myself to express to you what so many of us feel."

Roxie rolled her eyes, but closed the ledger, put down her pen and sat back in her chair, prepared to listen. She really didn't have time for this, but it was obvious that the only way she would get rid of him was to let him have his say. Only then would she have the pleasure of showing him the door.

"I can certainly understand your . . . commitment to an employee you've personally hired. A rash act," he digressed, "that I still firmly believe to be a mistake you'll one day come to rue."

"Luke has been doing very well." Since Fesol wouldn't say his name, she would. "And Gary tells me he's quite pleased with Luke's work." There, she'd said it twice.

"For now."

"For almost two months now," she corrected him.

Fesol pushed his glasses up the thin bridge of his nose and regarded her balefully through the thick lenses. "Well, that's neither here nor there. What I wished to say is that you've apparently allowed your compassion"—he made the term sound like some dreaded social disease—"to obscure your good sense. You've carried things too far."

Even while telling herself she had nothing to defend, she protested. "I can't see the harm in a few lunches, Fesol."

"You've had lunch with him four days in a row," he pointed out. "Four days, Roxie."

"Guilty as charged," she said flippantly.

Fesol drew his chin back into his neck like a turtle pulling in its head. "Already you're being unduly influenced."

Her fingers itched to pick up her pen and hurl it at him. From some mysterious source, however, she managed to retrieve a shred of patience and leave the writing instrument in place. With cold politeness, she said, "Are you through yet?"

He wasn't. "You are young and trusting. I merely wished to

warn you against permitting yourself to mistake your sympathetic concern for this . . . employee . . . to be anything more than what it is."

"Thank you for the warning, Fesol," she said through her teeth. "I assure you I'll give it all the consideration it deserves."

At that he removed himself from her desk. He ran a hand over the brown wisps of his hair and heaved a sigh. "I don't suppose you'll listen to me," he said in a gloomy tone, "but I felt I had to speak up. Everyone who works with you, everyone who knows you, shares my concern. An innocent young woman like you involving herself with a man like—"

"Yes, well, I appreciate your concern," Roxie cut in briskly. Standing, she walked to the door, opened it and held it wide. "Do, please, convey my appreciation to everyone else as well."

Shaking his head at the hopelessness of it all, Fesol left. Roxie slammed the door behind him, wishing she'd let herself throw the pen after all. Maybe her typewriter, too. Storming back to her desk, she flung herself into her chair and inhaled deeply. After the fifth big breath, she calmed a bit. Another couple of breaths and she began to giggle. Solicitous advice from Fesol Vernal of all people. It was a wonder he hadn't started in on the dangers of the birds and the bees!

Her laughter pealed as she pictured Fesol lecturing her on the birds and the bees and the hazards of mixing the two. She could just see him pausing to wipe steam from the lenses of his glasses and nearly choked. Wait until she told Luke!

Now her laughter died a quick death. No, this was one thing she wouldn't be telling Luke. Although she'd come to realize he had a strong sense of humor, she didn't think he would find Fesol's dire warnings the least bit amusing. And they weren't.

As much as she hated to admit it, Fesol was right about one thing. She had placed herself on the outside. She had made herself a target for the collective censure of her coworkers. She had done so from the moment she packed that first lunch for Luke. And with every day that passed, every lunch that the two of them shared, she slipped further and further away from the circle of acceptance.

But Roxie really didn't care. What she gained in those few hours with Luke more than made up for anything she may have lost. Bit by bit, a friendship was blossoming, a special kind of friendship.

Though they shied away from the type of deeply personal revelations that had marked their earliest discussions, every other subject was fair game—including the normally taboo subjects of politics and religion. They found they agreed more often than not, and on those occasions they teasingly congratulated each other on having such good sense. As she came to know more of him, Roxie became increasingly impatient to know everything about him. She felt rather as if she were on a treasure hunt, digging up the most unexpected prizes.

She learned he was well-read in everything from poetry to pulp fiction. Over yesterday's lunch of ham sandwiches and pineapple upside-down cake, he confessed that he had even begun reading the Bible his grandfather had left him. Rather sheepishly he said, "Maybe if I'd read it earlier . . ."

"It's never too late," she assured him.

He flashed her a rueful grin. "I hope you're right."

She learned he had old-fashioned values. He believed strongly in the bonds of marriage and family. He had strict views on fidelity and familial responsibility that had momentarily surprised her. Later, she'd realized it really shouldn't surprise her. Given his background, given his lack of family support, she understood just how important family would be to him.

Sometimes they were serious, like the day she asked him about the friends he'd made in prison.

He shrugged. "There weren't any."

"But surely in all those years—"

"You can't get attached in prison." His silvery eyes went steely gray as he looked at her like he was doing so from a long, long way away. "It's a transient world. The faces are always changing. And once somebody's gone, they're out of your life. Former prisoners aren't permitted to communicate with the ones still inside. So you learn not to get attached."

She lowered her head, trying to hide the grief she felt at all those years he'd had to suffer without someone to lean on.

But she couldn't hide anything from Luke. He chucked her under the chin and drawled lightly, "Does this mean you're sorry to hear I'm unattached?"

"Utterly devastated," she'd managed to say with a laugh. But of course, she wasn't sorry about it at all. And later she found herself wishing that he'd let his finger linger a little longer under her chin.

Sometimes they were not so serious, like the day he told her about the time he'd sharpened a stick and poked at one of his grandfather's bee hives. "Those bees came out of there, buzzing like saws gone berserk, and chased me up a tree."

"Did they sting you?" she asked.

"Hoo-boy, did they!" he said with a playful wince. He pointed to that sliver of a scar that stood out so whitely on his tanned cheek, a scar she had assumed he'd earned in a fight. "I was sitting on a branch of the tree, alternately swatting at them with the stick and covering my head and face as they swarmed me. Then I lost my balance, fell out of the tree and wound up cutting my face on the point of the stick."

She gasped. "Oh, that must have hurt like the dickens!"

"It did."

"I'll bet your grandfather was horrified."

He made a face. "Furious is more like it."

She did a double-take. "Furious? Why?"

"Because I killed so many of his bees, for one."

"Which meant they couldn't pollinate the fruit trees."

"Or make honey," he added.

"And for another?"

"Because it ruined that hive and it had to be rebuilt."

"Well," she said in a mock-schoolmarm's voice, "I hope you learned your lesson."

"Let's just say that by the time they tired of stinging me and I stopped bleeding, I had developed a very healthy respect for Granddad's bees," he admitted with a quick grin.

Their ringing laughter produced a round of silence among their coworkers, but Roxie didn't care. So long as she could hear Luke's laughter, she didn't care what anyone else thought. She had remembered him as a young man filled with a love of life and laugher. His enjoyment in life had been suppressed, submerged beneath a defensive detachment. Gradually his true personality was reemerging, and she was fascinated by the transformation.

Thinking of transformations, Roxie shook herself out of her reveries and onto her feet. She should have left fifteen minutes ago. Those Ladies Aide members who were free this evening were meeting in the church basement to bake their goods for the sale tomorrow, and she still had to stop by the Blue Ridge General Store to buy a can of molasses before she joined them.

But first she needed to put the completed ledger on Layton Stewart's desk. Normally he was the first one in of a morning and the last one to leave in the evening. Today, though, he'd left at noon so he could pick up his wife and drive her to St. Joseph to stay and help their daughter care for their newborn grandbaby now that mother and son had been released from the hospital. Even so, he would expect to find the ledger waiting for him when he returned on Monday.

She entered his office just as Barbara McCanse laid some letters on his desk.

"Oh, hi," the pretty blonde secretary said, looking a little hesitant.

"You're here late." Roxie hoped she sounded casual.

Barbara shrugged. "I wanted to finish typing these letters so Mr. Stewart can sign them first thing Monday morning."

"I see." Roxie set the ledger next to the letters. "Have you got the bank packet?"

"Mr. Stewart gave it to me before he left. I'll put it in the night deposit slot on my way home."

"Well, have a good weekend," Roxie said and turned to leave.

"About you and Luke Bauer."

Roxie froze in the doorframe.

"I don't care what Willie or Fesol say, I think he's okay," Barbara declared in a rush. "He works hard and doesn't cause any trouble. Besides, he's a real good-looker. And if any man ever set eyes on me the way he does on you, I wouldn't care what he'd done either."

Though she was sorely tempted, Roxie managed not to smile or laugh or do anything undignified. She merely nodded and said, "I'll see you Monday" and left the warehouse.

But the encounter buoyed her. As they had after she'd hired him, people would gradually come to accept him. She believed that with all her heart. She whistled cheerily as she drove back to town and carried the tune with her when she parked in front of the general store.

The long bench outside the store was empty, which meant she didn't have to stop to visit with anyone—a welcome change. In the summer, the iceman made a delivery three times a week to leave fifty pounds of ice in the big square soda cooler that stood on the porch next to the door. Those who could afford it bought a soda to sip as they sat there talking about their crops or the weather or their neighbors. Those who could not afford a soda dipped into the cooler and took a chunk of ice to suck on. This summer, it was rumored, there had been more ice taken than soda sold.

Inside the store, Roxie was greeted with conversations dwindling into dead silence and grazing glances of chilling brevity. It was a curt reminder that acceptance wouldn't come as easily as she had hoped.

"Hello," she said to one and all.

Agnes Dill sniffed audibly and jammed the package of headache powder she had just purchased into her handbag.

Two women who had been visiting with each other nodded brusquely and turned away to finish their shopping.

The four men who were sitting around the long-range radio in the back of the store and talking over the announcer probably didn't hear her.

Virginia Jones stepped out from behind the old-fashioned brass cash register and hurried over to give Roxie a quick hug. "How can I help you, dear?"

Though she half-suspected Virginia's action stemmed more from a desire to further ruffle Agnes's feathers than to soothe her own, Roxie nonetheless gave her a grateful smile. "I need to buy a can of molasses."

"Are you making those good cookies of yours?"

Roxie nodded. "The Ladies Aide is meeting in the church kitchen this evening to do the baking."

"It ought to be a little cooler there, being in the basement."

"I certainly hope so."

As Agnes swept past them and out of the store, Virginia added fuel to the nosy parker's fire. "Be sure to save a few of your cookies for Luke."

Roxie knew exactly what the older woman was doing, and it took everything she had not to laugh. "He said he'd try to come to the sale."

"Oh, I'll bet he'll be there with bells on." Before she turned away to help another customer, Virginia added, "Just take what you need, dear. I have to work tomorrow, so that will be my contribution."

"Thank you." In a much better mood now, Roxie went in search of her molasses.

The store was dimly lit, smelled not unpleasantly of leather and peppermint and tobacco, and was crammed with the necessities of life. A counter ran the length of one wall. In addition to the cash register, it was covered with bottles of patent medicines, a large scale for measuring, glass jars filled with penny candies, pickled eggs, or pickles. Barrels of crackers, kegs of nails and sacks of chicken feed stood at the end of shelves that ran floor to ceiling and were stuffed with everything from shoes to pharmaceuticals to yard goods to groceries.

As she neared the back, a radio bulletin came in about a break-out from the federal penitentiary in Leavenworth, Kansas, immediately followed by a description of the car the jailbirds had stolen after making their escape.

"I wonder which way they're headed," one of the men said.

"The announcer said they're from Chicago," a second man supplied.

"Which means they're probably on their way north now," somebody else speculated.

"Yeah, well, we've got our own homegrown convict to worry about," the fourth man sniped.

Roxie stopped right then and almost said something. She thought of Luke, who hadn't missed a day of work since he started and who was doing his best to make up for what he readily admitted were his stupid mistakes. Instead, she grabbed her small can of molasses off the shelf and left the store with nary a word.

"You're awfully quiet this evening."

Roxie pulled her last sheet of cookies out of the oven and, straightening, smiled at Lottie Campbell. "It was a busy week at work, so I guess I'm still a little tired."

"I certainly understand." Lottie lifted a hand to push a damp strand of her dark hair back from her brow. She was expecting her first child any day now and could easily have pleaded her late-term pregnancy as an excuse not to participate tonight. But her railroad detective husband was working the Wichita run and wouldn't be home until tomorrow morning, so she had volunteered to help clean up after the baking marathon.

And a marathon, it was. After sharing a light supper of tuna salad and quartered tomatoes in the social hall, the Ladies Aide group had swooped in and taken over the church kitchen with its wide counters, oversized ovens and deep double sinks. They'd stirred cake batter, rolled pie crusts, chopped various fruits and nuts and dropped spoonfuls of cookie dough until the baked goods they hoped to sell covered every available surface. Now they were just about finished cleaning up their mess.

Roxie turned the nearest floor fan toward her friend, hoping to stir up a little more cool air to offset the warmth from the ovens. "It must be rough being pregnant in this heat."

"That's putting it mildly." Lottie snatched a molasses cookie off the cooling rack and then gave Roxie an arch look. "Just wait until you find some nice young man to marry. See what you have to look forward to?"

The innocent statement seemed to have a hidden message. Roxie examined Lottie's shiny face and decided her suspicions were groundless. She was becoming paranoid. Lottie didn't mean anything.

Just the same, depression crept in on Roxie. Finding a "nice young man" wasn't as easy as it sounded. She knew. She'd tried. Now she was beginning to wonder if she ever would. All of her high school friends and most of her college classmates were married, many of them with young children already. She was well past what Blue Ridge considered the normal marriageable age and could, she supposed, be called a spinster.

No sooner had Lottie carried Roxie's used cookie sheet and spatula to the suds-filled sink to wash it than Candise Sherman chimed in. "Do you remember my friend Robertha, Robertha Homan?"

Roxie thought a minute. "Vaguely, yes."

"Well, her cousin Ralph has been accepted into veterinary school at the University of Missouri."

"That's nice."

Candise centered her blackberry jam cake on a doily-covered plate. "He's going to be in town for a couple of weeks before he starts school, staying with Robertha and her husband."

Involuntarily, Roxie's stance took on a defensive rigidity. "What's this all about, Candise? Are you trying to fix me up?"

"Not if you're not interested," she replied, unperturbed. "But if you should decide you might be—"

"Thanks, but no thanks," Roxie responded as pleasantly as she could. It was quite a feat, as she wasn't feeling very pleasant.

"She's waiting for Charles 'Buddy' Rogers to fly in on that airplane of his from *Wings*," Roxie's sister-in-law Marlene said with a smirk.

"Or for Tom Mix to come riding into town on his horse Tony," Ola Barber said on a titter.

Candise shrugged. "Well, if you change your mind—"

The preacher's wife, Margaret Pierce, came to Roxie's rescue, clapping her hands and saying, "It's going on eight o'clock, ladies, and we have an early day tomorrow, so let's finish getting the kitchen cleaned up and get home."

By the time all the baking utensils were washed and dried and put neatly away, Roxie sensed a conspiracy in the making. Having happened, said Julia Murphy, to overhear Candise mention Robertha's cousin Ralph, she couldn't help relating that she'd met him at a Christmas party last year.

"Such a nice young man," she declared.

"A nice young man," Rose Dirks echoed.

The phrase caught Roxie's ear. She darted a look at Ola, who was in deep discussion with Elsie Martin as they hung their damp towels to dry on the metal hooks above the double sinks. Perhaps she wasn't paranoid after all.

Within five minutes she was certain she wasn't. Elsie came first, stepping into place beside Roxie and complaining that she was exhausted. "Thank heaven we're finished," she whined, then quickly added, "But you must be really worn out—after working all day at the warehouse and all."

"It's not any more tiring than housework, Elsie."

"No, not physically, but you've got to deal with so many problems."

"You've got a point, Elise," Ola agreed. "Why, I wouldn't want Roxie's job for anything, having to handle all the responsibilities she does." She gave Roxie a look brimming with sympathetic understanding. "You made a tough decision when you took on Luke Bauer. It must take a lot out of you to stand by it."

Roxie let it pass as she checked her apron for stains. Finding none, she folded it and put it away in the designated drawer. The pattern was beginning to take shape. Divert her with a "nice young man," then stress the not-so-niceness of the one threatening her, sweetened by a heavy dose of compassion. Her first reaction was sheer anger. At least Fesol had had the courage to tell her outright, even if he did dress it up as "friendly advice."

But, as always, her wrath was fleeting. Fesol hadn't been exaggerating when he'd said everyone was concerned. She could see it in their eyes, in the way each of them found it so difficult to speak to her. It touched her, this comprehensive caring about what happened to her. Even as she resented the interference, Roxie felt moved by the solicitude.

In a welter of confusion, she welcomed the end of the evening. She boxed up her cookies so the transportation committee could move them to the bank tomorrow and then made her good-nights hurriedly before escaping up the stairs. She wasn't quite fast enough, however. Marlene reached her side before she reached the top.

"Hold on a minute, Roxie," her sister-in-law said. "I'd like a word with you."

Thoroughly tired, feeling as if she'd been plowed under a ton of conflicting emotions, she wanted nothing less than to hear another word about men, nice or otherwise. "Some other time, Marlene. Please, I'm exhausted."

"I won't keep you long. I just want to ask you to think about what you're doing."

Roxie blew out a long, bitter breath. Hadn't she already heard this lecture? But she didn't evade the point. "A few lunches together. What's so awful about that? All we've done is talk."

"It's what those talks will lead to that worries us."

"You expect us to tear off our clothes and make love on the tabletops?"

A flash of hurt clouded Marlene's expression. "Of course not. But for your own good, don't forget what he is."

"He doesn't have leprosy. His past isn't contagious!" Roxie couldn't hold in her exasperation.

"We don't care about his past, dear, can't you see that? We don't care about him at all. It's you we care about, you and your future." Marlene clasped her sister-in-law's shoulders and gently shook her. "We love you, and we don't want to see you hurt. We don't ever again want to see you looking like the whipped puppy you were when you came back from St. Louis. So, please, think about those innocent little lunches and just what exactly you're getting into. Okay?"

Roxie's heart knocked painfully against her ribcage. It seemed to take a lifetime for the word to come to her lips. But inevitably, it did. "Okay."

On the heels of her promise, she broke free of Marlene's grasp and bolted up the last of the stairs.

Roxie kept to her word. She thought about it. In fact, she thought of little else the rest of the weekend. With careful deliberation she assessed the value of the hints and warnings she'd received. She easily dismissed the common fears that Luke was either a dangerous man or a villainous one. Despite what he'd done nearly eight years ago, Luke was industrious, reliable, determined to reshape his life. She knew no one would believe it, but he was far more conservative than she, even on legal issues. No, she wasn't worried about Luke's past, nor even about his possible recidivism.

She was worried about Luke the man. The sensitive, intelligent, gentle man who could make her heart sing with his laughter and sigh with his quietude. And now she was worried about herself.

More than anything Marlene had said, it had been the remark about the whipped puppy that caused Roxie to seriously ponder what she might be getting herself into. As much as it galled her to admit it, she had returned from St. Louis with her head hung and her tail between her legs. She'd been broken emotionally—at the time, she thought irreparably—but time truly does heal all wounds, and as she mended she'd clung to the certain resolution that she'd never again allow herself to be so hurt.

121

In the past few weeks that resolution had been endangered. Even in such a short time, she'd revealed far more of herself to Luke than she ever had to Arthur. She'd made herself vulnerable to Luke as she had never done with another man, and all because Luke was the one thing Arthur had never been—her friend. And she treasured his friendship.

If friendship were all she felt for Luke, she would defy the whole town, the whole world if necessary, to preserve it. If friendship were all, she wouldn't give a fingersnap for anyone's opinion.

But unable to lie to herself, Roxie admitted it wasn't all. She felt more, far more, for him. She'd been attracted to him from the first, from the day he'd walked into her office—no, even before that, from the moment she'd seen him walking down Main Street on the day he had arrived. Her heart had pumped wildly, and she hadn't been able to take her eyes off him. She had wondered even then what it would be like to touch the man behind the austere mask.

The more she came to know him, the more she wanted to know how he would feel beneath her caress, how he would taste upon her lips, how he would look in unrestrained passion. She often recalled the night she'd hurt her ankle, the warmth of his arms encircling her, the way his breath had stirred her hair, and she would ache with longing for more. Each time he touched her, each brief grazing of fingertips or light brush of his arm, deepened her hunger to know what comfort, what passion, what joy lay within the warmth of his embrace, within the heat of his kiss.

More often now, she saw an answering need within his darkening gaze, and with it she knew they were moving slowly, inexorably, irrevocably, beyond friendship.

For all that she was willing to be Luke's friend, Roxie wasn't ready to risk anything deeper. Her emotional scars were still painfully visible, too much so. Maybe later on she could take another chance on love, but not now, not yet. She had to back away while she still could, with her heart whole.

Her decision seemed preordained. She pleaded a blinding headache on Saturday morning as an excuse not to work the bake sale. She even missed church on Sunday, more because she was sick at heart than achy of head as she had claimed the day before.

By the time she returned to work and entered the lunchroom on Monday, Roxie felt as if this ending had been destined from the beginning. She had dressed for the occasion, wearing a drab navy-blue shirtwaist that she had dug out of the back of her closet and clipping her hair back off her face. Neither the dress nor the hairstyle really became her, but they gave her a protective aura of reserve. She wished she could as easily have donned a shield for her heart.

Luke waited for her at what had become their table. Unlike the cautious restraint that had marked his first greetings of her, he met her with an open cordiality marked by one of his charmingly lopsided smiles. Unable to confront the allure of his smile or the expectation in his eyes, she dropped her gaze to the floor. As he always did, he stood and pulled a chair out for her.

"Are you feeling better?" he asked.

His question startled her into looking up at him. "Feel—? Oh, yes, thank you. I just had a headache."

"That's what they told me at the bake sale," he said, not seeming to notice that she remained standing.

"You did go to the sale then?"

"I bought the last half-dozen of your molasses cookies and brought one for each of us for dessert today."

Gathering all her courage, Roxie delivered the speech she had rehearsed. "I'm sorry, Luke. I can't stay for lunch. I've got a pile of work on my desk that I need to take care of."

Luke felt his smile slowly melt away. Disappointment flooded him. These lunches had become the highlight of his day, his life. But acutely aware of the gaggle of gossipy coworkers who made up their audience, he managed a credible nonchalance. "Ah, well, tomorrow then."

"I'm sorry, I can't tomorrow either," she said.

He took in the dreary dress, the dispassionate demeanor, and his heart began to thud sickeningly. Dear God, no, not this, anything but this. He'd been so careful, so damned careful not to expect more. But he was totally unprepared to receive less. He couldn't bear it. He couldn't believe it. He wouldn't believe it.

"Maybe next week," he tried.

"Maybe," she agreed.

But they both knew the word had no meaning.

# Chapter 8

Dirt smudged her cheek and forearm, and sweat dampened her back. Her hair was hidden under the scarf she'd tied atop her head, leaving the ends rabbit-eared. The beige of her cap-sleeved blouse had been bleached to an off-white, and the brown of her wide-legged slacks was faded to a drab dun. A passer-by might think she looked like a ragamuffin.

But Luke thought Roxie looked as cute as a button and sexy as all get-out.

He watched her from a distance, from beneath one of the large maple trees that lined the street and cast pretty patterns of light and shadow over all. He watched, and his whole being suffered the stirring torment of desire as she finished yanking weeds from the garden that flanked the front walk. She stood, picked up a large metal watering can and began pouring its contents on the pots of flowers that climbed the steps to the porch. He'd thought he wouldn't want her so much, not now, not after the pain he'd endured. He'd thought he'd deadened every possible emotion he could conceivably feel for her.

But he'd been wrong. He wanted her more than ever before. He throbbed with the wanting. He wanted to touch her, to glide his hands over her curves, to press himself against her softness, to ease his aching within her. In all his life he'd never wanted a woman the way he wanted Roxie.

It went beyond wanting. He needed her. He needed her gentleness, her kindness, her sweet humor. It made him feel sick, this wanting and needing. He couldn't have her. He could never have her. He hadn't even been able to keep her as a friend. She had come to her senses.

And with a single "maybe" she'd crushed his spirit, as a lifetime with little affection or acceptance had not been able to do, as seven long years in prison had not been able to do.

He didn't question why Roxie had brought such an abrupt end to their lunches, why she'd severed their growing friendship. He had no doubt why. She had finally realized what everyone else already knew, that he wasn't the sort of man she should be encouraging, however innocently. He had to acknowledge that on his part it had never been so innocent. He'd wanted her friendship, yes, but even more he'd hungered for her as a man craves a woman. He'd filled every fantasy with her image and with every fantasy his desire had grown. In some way he must have revealed his true feelings and frightened her away.

The watering completed, she stretched, arching her back and tipping her head first to the right and then to the left, and his heart thumped violently. He forced himself to look elsewhere. A car backed out of a driveway down the street and turned toward uptown. He considered riding away as quietly as he'd arrived on the old motorcycle he'd recently purchased, but pride kept him from leaving. He'd come with a purpose and could not leave before he'd accomplished what he'd set out to do.

After dismounting, he plucked the jar he'd brought off the sidecar seat and crossed the street.

Even before she heard his footsteps coming up the walk, Roxie stood still, the empty watering can in her hand. With a prickling certainty, she felt his approach. She gulped in a breath, set the watering can down, and slowly pivoted on her heels.

"Hello, Roxie," he said.

"Hello, Luke." She shielded her eyes with a hand and watched him come up the walk.

His dark hair was tousled and seemed to absorb the sunlight that struck it. He had on an old blue chambray shirt that was missing the top buttons, exposing the tanned column of his throat and a fair portion of his chest, and he'd rolled the sleeves of it up to his elbows. The legs of his washed-out jeans ended at a pair of black boots she hadn't seen him wear before.

He stopped just a few feet from her and stood stiffly, his face closed, his gaze remote. Her heart gave an odd little lurch. She lowered her hand, and they faced each other in an awkward silence.

"What brings you to this part of town?" she finally asked, sounding stilted.

"I'm not allowed in this part of town?"

"No, that wasn't what I . . ." Flushing, she let her words trail off and dropped her gaze to the ground.

Luke silently swore. There was no sense trying to deny it. He had hoped for something else. He'd hoped for his own confident charm and her sweet smiles. He'd longed for a warm reception, not this wooden restraint. It was obvious she'd sooner receive heat stroke than him. He couldn't deny his biting disappointment. He had wished for a miracle, but he should have known better. A childhood of wishing had brought him nothing but a manhood of emptiness.

Aimlessly kicking a small pebble with the toe of her oxford, Roxie chided herself. How could she sound so unwelcoming to him? How could she, when her heart was leaping with the joy of seeing him? Even if she didn't want to get involved with him, she could at least be cordial. Simple courtesy demanded it. The pebble rolled into the green of the grass, and she returned her attention to him.

"Well, I'm glad you stopped by to say hello. It seems like I never get a chance to see you at work anymore." She wondered if her statements sounded as false to him as they did to her.

Luke didn't know which was worse, her lifeless reserve or this artificial congeniality. "It's hard when we're both so busy."

"Yes, it is," she agreed a little too quickly.

He was sorry he'd come. It had all been for a stupid, prideful gesture—and an even more imbecilic hope. He decided to save them both any further embarrassment and leave. "Well, I should get moving."

She caught sight of the jar in his hand. "What's that?" she asked, pointing, and he heartily cursed himself for bringing it, for coming here, for putting himself through all this pain. She was still staring at the jar. He had no choice now but to give it to her.

"It's for you," he said, thrusting it at her. "You never let me repay you for all the lunches you brought me. I thought this would clear the debt."

Her mouth softened into a smile as she took the jar from him and studied its liquid amber contents. "Honey?"

"From my grandfather's hives," he confirmed. "I inherited three jars of it along with his Bible. You said once that you remembered how good his honey was on your mother's biscuits, and I thought you might enjoy having some again."

"Oh, I will," she assured him.

"The jar is sealed with beeswax from the comb to help keep the honey from turning to sugar."

Roxie smiled directly at him now, both hands curled around the glass. His gift had touched her deeply. Mainly because it meant he remembered her saying how much she liked his grandfather's honey. But she was grateful for far more than the honey. She was glad, so glad just to see him again.

"Thank you, Luke, but you don't owe me for those lunches,"

He shrugged, sending his shoulder muscles into play beneath the material of his shirt. "In any event, we're even now, so I guess I'll just—"

"You'll come in for some lemonade to cool you off," she interrupted. Simple courtesy be hanged. He was here, and she wanted him to stay.

Thinking nothing would cool him off around her, Luke looked away and caught a slight movement of the neighbor's curtain that told him they were the objects of someone's curiosity. "Is anyone home?"

"Me," she said with a laugh.

"I meant anyone else."

She shook her head. "Mother serves lunch at the county orphanage on Saturdays, so Dad usually meets my brothers for a bite at Sanders Café after he closes the bank."

The curtains parted now and Luke saw a nose pressed against the neighbor's window. "I probably shouldn't come in if you're here alone."

Roxie finally understood when she followed the direction of his gaze. She scowled at the neighbor woman watching them out her window. Then her scowl turned into a smile as she waved him toward the front steps.

"Oh, come on," she said, "let's give that nosy old Mrs. Cutter something juicy to talk about."

"Juicy?"

Roxie saw that his lidded gaze couldn't conceal the wicked glint in his eyes. Flummoxed by that glint, she bent over and deadheaded a potted geranium.

"Okay," he agreed, his lightness of tone relieving her discomfort. "Let's do that."

They walked up the steps to the porch. Her hands full, she paused, and he reached around her to open the door. Her pulse raced as memory sparked. They'd come this way before, but then she'd been in his arms, snuggled against his heart, the warmth and strength of him thrilling her as even the mere memory did. She knew a wish that he would remember, too.

Luke's body pulsated as he remembered the night he'd entered with her in his arms. He could still smell her subtle rosewater scent, could still hear the soft catch in her breath when she tried to stand on her own, could still feel the bittersweet pleasure of her delicate curves held captive in his arms. The memory excited him, and he strove to forget.

Inside, the house was as clean and cool as he remembered it. She led him through the dining room into an immaculate kitchen, and he was filled with new longing. He wished he'd left when he'd had the chance. What the hell had prompted him to accept her invitation? What had prompted her to issue it?

Roxie fanned her face with her hands and blew straggling wisps of hair that had escaped the scarf off her brow. Luke's handsome features were darkened by a sadness, and it wounded her to see it. More than anything else, she longed to see his smile, hear his husky laughter. She wanted to see the life return to his eyes. She could not let him leave looking like this.

"I'm glad you showed up," she said, setting the jar he'd given her on the oilcloth-covered table and tossing the faded flower into the trash. "Not just because of the honey, though I can't wait to try it, but because it's too hot to be weeding today."

Though she gave him an opportunity to speak, Luke said nothing. She raised her arms to her head and untied the scarf holding up her hair. It rippled free, and she shook it loosely about her shoulders. Then she took her time about finger-combing it off her face. Every moment was agonizingly delightful. Just being near her, inhaling her scent that today held a kick of garden green, watching the fluid beauty of her motions, listening to each breath she drew, pleasured him. But it was a painful pleasure, knowing it was the last time for him to be with her like this. He couldn't allow himself to hope for more. Hope so often led to disappointment.

"Let me pour you some lemonade," she offered after washing

and drying her hands.

"Just a quick glass," he said. "I really need to get moving."

She took two glasses out of the cupboard, then a full-to-the-brim pitcher out of the icebox. After chipping some ice off the block in a bowl on the top shelf, she poured their drinks. Watching her, it was all he could do not to touch her. Even in her mussed state, she looked so touchable and soft. He wondered if she would run screaming out the front door if he took her in his arms and kissed her the way he longed to.

"Where are you going?" she asked as she handed him his glass.

He drained his lemonade in one long, thirsty swallow and then set his empty glass in the sink. "Out to look at my grand-father's old place."

"That's an awfully long walk," she said, and sipped her cold lemonade.

"Oh, I'm not walking."

"You have a car?"

"A motorcycle."

She blinked. "A motorcycle! Where did you get a motorcycle?"

"I'm buying it from my landlady," he explained. "Her husband rode motorcycles in the war and he bought one when he came home. A year or so later he fell off the roof of a barn he was helping a friend build and died, and she just left it where he'd parked it, in the shed behind the boardinghouse. It needs some work, so I started tinkering with it and discovered that the motor still runs. Hums like one of the sewing machine she keeps in the spare room, in fact. When I asked her about it, she said she'd sell it to me for a good price and that she'd let me pay it off by doing odd jobs that she doesn't have to hire out."

"Like painting the porch." She remembered him saying he had to do that before he could go to the bake sale.

"And washing all the windows and putting up screens," he

added. "And replacing the flattened tin cans covering the holes in the roof with real shingles. You name it, I'm doing it."

"A motorcycle is certainly cheaper than a car," she commented, thinking of all the money she'd spent these last few months to keep hers in good running condition.

"It uses a lot less gas, too." He turned to leave. "Well, thanks for the lemonade."

Oh, no. He wasn't getting away from her that easily, Roxie thought. Leaving her half-full glass on the table, she followed him out of the house, down the stairs and across the street. She'd never seen a motorcycle in person, only in magazines or at the movies, and she wasn't sure what to expect. It looked a lot like a bicycle, only bigger and heavier, with rubber grips and metal gears on the handle bars and a saddle-style seat for the rider. She walked around it, studying the faded red paint that covered it from front to back and the rust spots that speckled the rounded fuel tank.

Her expression must have given her away because he said, "I'm going to sand it and paint it first chance I get."

She rolled her bottom lip between her teeth as she searched. "Where's the brake?"

He pointed to the single drum fitted to the rear wheel. "Right there."

Now she nodded at what appeared to be a small, open-topped dirigible attached to the motorcycle by two metal rods—one in the front and one in the back. "What's that?"

"The sidecar." When she just looked at him blankly, he elaborated. "It's where the passenger rides. See, it's even got a little door and a windshield."

She stepped closer to study the contraption.

"I'd be glad to give you a ride in it," he went on, "but I'm sure you've got better things to do."

"No, actually, I don't." A brazen feeling broke free inside her, a derring-do that had long been locked up in her chest. "And I've never ridden in a motorcycle sidecar before."

The hope Luke had been trying to suppress no longer would be restrained. It surged through his entire being. Maybe, just maybe, he was being given a second chance to gain her friendship.

"Well, we can certainly rectify that." Like a gentleman of old, he bent at the waist and opened that little door for her. "Your carriage awaits, Miss Mitchell."

Laughing at his antics, Roxie climbed into the sidecar and plopped down on the wooden seat. "What do I do now?"

"Just relax and enjoy the ride," he instructed as he mounted the motorcycle.

Her heart pounded with anticipation when he kick-started the engine. It didn't roar but rather purred like a large cat. Sitting in the sidecar, she could feel the thrum of it up through her shoe soles and the seat. The vibration was surprisingly thrilling.

She gripped the edge of the sidecar as they pulled away from the curb. Then she remembered Mrs. Cutter and, feeling a bit impudent, turned and waved at the neighbor's window as they glided down the street. A bubble of laughter burst on her lips when she saw the curtains snap closed.

The looks they got as they circled the block were priceless. Eyes popped and jaws dropped. She smiled and waved at everyone they passed, but most of them were too shocked to smile or wave back. Too soon, it seemed, they were rounding her corner.

Slowing the motorcycle as they neared her house, Luke said, "Are you ready to go home?"

Roxie's head was buzzing with excitement but she shook it emphatically. "I want to see The Bee Man's place."

He shot her a quizzical look. "The Bee Man?"

"That's what my mother used to call your grandfather."

"Okay, then, hang on," he said.

She did, gripping the other side of the car with her free hand, and away they went.

The sun and the hot wind beat at them mercilessly as they passed the boardinghouse where he lived and the fairgrounds where the town's annual carnival was running full bore, before hitting a smooth stretch of blacktop. A shuddering jiggle rose up through the floor and the seat beneath her when he turned onto an old gravel road that spewed a choking coat of dust all over them and blew dried vegetation into the ditch. Discomfort aside, she couldn't remember the last time she'd had this much fun.

"How do you like it?" he shouted at her.

"I love it!"

A half-mile or so later, the motorcycle swerved to the side of the road and stopped.

"There it is," Luke said, and cut the engine.

"This is where your grandfather lived?" Roxie asked in a low voice.

"Yep." Luke tried to see it through her eyes, and all he could think was that it was a sad sight to behold. "I guess it just got to be too much for him to keep up with in his final years."

It certainly looked that way, thought Luke. The fieldstone house sat at the end of a long dirt and rock-strewn drive. The roof was in dire need of repair, the brick chimney was lopsided, and the shutters hung slightly askew. The grass in the front yard had died, a bag swing that had lost its stuffing hung limply from a tree limb, and the few wooden fence rails and posts that remained were both weather-beaten and termite-eaten.

The orchard that stood on a small rise to the side of the house wasn't in any better shape. Oh, the trees were laden with peaches ready for the picking and apples coming on strong but it was only a matter of time before they went to rot. And the trees themselves looked as if they desperately needed a good pruning. All told, the once-thriving grove appeared to be going back to the wild for lack of attention.

Luke climbed off the motorcycle and then helped Roxie alight from the sidecar. "You might be a little off-balance at first, so hold onto me until you feel steady enough to stand on your own."

He was right. Roxie felt her knees nearly buckle beneath her. It took her a moment to regain her equilibrium while she clutched his arm. She let go of him then with a heartfelt, "Thank you."

He turned his attention back to that ramshackle house and the untended grounds that surrounded it. "I know it doesn't look it now," he said, "but at one time this was a place to be proud of."

Realizing her hair must look frightful, she smoothed it down as best she could. "I remember hearing once that your grandfather was one of the earliest residents of Blue Ridge."

"He pioneered this land, homesteading in an old lean-to while he cleared it. Then he built the house from the rocks he'd dug up and the bee hives from the trees he'd cut down."

"Did he plant the fruit trees?"

"Plotted the orchard and planted the trees."

"Then he married your grandmother." She stated the obvious.

He nodded. "I don't remember her—she died shortly after giving birth to my mother. And I only have a vague recollection of my mother because she left when I was still in short pants. But Granddad was a stubborn old coot." The corners of his mouth lifted a bit at that last. "He had offers to sell over the years but he always said he wouldn't leave his bees or his trees, so he lived here until he died."

"When was that?"

"Eight months before I got out of prison."

And just a couple months before she'd come home, she realized. Brushing off her clothes, she turned to a more pleasant topic. "I'll bet you loved coming out here."

"I hated going back to my father's house." His voice went a shade raspy, as if some of the gravel dust had collected on his vocal chords.

She pulled her handkerchief out of the front pocket of her slacks and used it to wipe off her face. "I wonder who lives here now."

"Nobody, from the looks of it."

Raking his fingers through his own tousled hair, Luke made a decision. He started up the drive, saying over his shoulder, "Wait here, I'm going to check things out."

But Roxie hadn't come all this way only to be left behind. She scrambled to catch up with him. "I'm going with you," she said.

The fecund scent of ripening fruit filled the air.

"Ah, the sweet smell of freedom," he said, inhaling deeply.

She could feel the fluttering of the pulse in her throat. She'd felt deliciously quivery ever since he'd arrived at her house, but now she felt dangerously so. She debated within herself, then, looking straight ahead, she murmured, "You were in prison an awfully long time."

Luke sighed. Back to this. It always came back to this. No matter how far he'd come, it seemed he couldn't escape the invisible bars of his past. He skimmed his gaze over her profile. Had this been behind their rift? If it were, he couldn't risk not answering her unspoken question.

"Yes," he said, "I was."

"Longer than usual?"

The quizzical look she gave him touched him, yet irritated him too. God, to be so unbelievably innocent! If it were any other woman, he'd be dead certain it was an act. But with Roxie he had no doubt it wasn't. And it irritated him because he believed her innocence set them irrevocably apart.

"I never made it easy on myself," he told her. "Not from the beginning. First I resisted arrest and then I refused to cooperate with the attorney my grandfather hired to defend me. Worse, I was rude to the judge. So rude, in fact, that he came down on me like a hammer at sentencing time."

The drive was long and narrow with huge oak trees hemming it in one side and weeds growing wild on the other. It narrowed at one point and they had to walk in single file, with him slowing to show her any rocks or tree roots in her path. He paused to hold back an overhanging tree limb, and she ducked under it with hushed agility, her body brushing close to his.

Trying not to notice either her body or his reaction to it, he let go of the limb and they resumed walking side by side as he finished telling her his story. "I guess I saw myself as some sort of noble loner, withstanding whatever punishment they threw my way. But I was just a scared and lonely kid acting like the tough guy I mistakenly imagined myself to be."

She jerked to a stop. As he halted beside her, she looked up at him and whispered, "I'm sorry, Luke."

He glanced down at her. Her fragile face was filled with concern, and knowing it was for him almost brought him to his knees. He was tempted, oh, so tempted, to reach over and stroke away her frown. His every nerve jumped with the longing to touch her. But he couldn't risk scaring her away again. And even though they stood close to each other, she was as far out of his reach as the moon.

"Don't be sorry for me, Roxie," he said, his voice sharp. Then he repeated in a softer tone, "Don't be. It's all over and done with, long ago. And you shouldn't waste your sympathy on someone who was as stupidly stubborn as I was. I'm solely to blame for putting myself behind bars."

"It takes a big man to admit that," she said with quiet admiration.

Once again, her sincerity almost proved his undoing. Desperate to change the subject, he broke off a small tree limb and stripped a leaf from it. "I hope you know you might be breaking the law."

That succeeded in turning her attention. "Breaking the law?"

He tossed the tree limb away and tapped her nose with the leaf. "If someone else owns this place now, we're trespassing."

The leaf tickled. She blew it and his warning away with a saucy, "Lead on, Clyde. Bonnie will follow."

Laughing together, they emerged from a cat's-cradle of light and shade into the heat of the sun. The sky held a mixture of blues, from near gray to vivid robin's egg, and was virtually cloudless with just the merest wraith of a white smudge floating occasionally by. A breeze gentled the air and birds glided away with it.

Walking beside him, Roxie could only wonder how she managed to move on legs that felt so unsteady. Her nerves seemed magnetized by his very nearness, crackling each time he drew a breath. She felt more alive than she had in days, years, yet at the same time she was oddly more at peace.

Luke felt the excruciating joy of being near Roxie. He sweetly tortured himself with visions of pulling her into his arms, kissing her senseless with all the pent-up need he felt, and caressing her into submission. He nearly groaned aloud. The frustration was enough to try a saint, much less a sinner like himself. Calling upon every fiber of strength he possessed, he forced the tantalizing images from his mind.

"I'm going to see how the beehives have fared," he said, feeling the need to put a little distance between them.

"Go ahead. I'll just look around here while I'm waiting."

Roxie made the effort to keep her voice light as Luke turned away from her. When he stood too close to her, when he looked at her in that peculiar, penetrating way of his, she couldn't breathe properly.

He strode off, and she watched him until he disappeared, swallowed up by the trees. The abandoned house drew her almost irresistibly. She wandered around it, peeking in windows at peeling wallpaper, dirty linoleum, a sagging pantry door, a rusted iron pump, and a hole in the wall where the cook stove was once vented. The gay profusion of tiger lilies growing willy-nilly around the perimeter of the backyard spoke to the fact that someone had once cared about the place. But now it was simply sad, for the dreams that might have been nurtured there were as dead as their dreamers.

Her mouth and throat were as dry as the dust she'd eaten on the motorcycle ride, so it was a relief to find that the metal pump near the back door still worked. She gave the handle a good draw then stuck her mouth under the spigot and guzzled the cold, clear well water that spouted out. When she'd drunk her fill, she wet her handkerchief and used it to wipe the dust and the sweat off her face.

Feeling somewhat refreshed, she stood in the doorway of a garage-like structure behind the house and looked around. A pith helmet with a protective veil hung from a nail on one wall and mason jars of every size sat on wooden shelves against another wall. Tools covered a bench in the middle of the room, and the gas burner standing near it told her that this was probably where Luke's grandfather had processed his honey.

When she had finished exploring, Roxie sat down on the back step to wait for Luke. He wasn't long in coming, and it was obvious from his expression that he was disappointed with what he'd seen. She gathered he wasn't quite ready to leave yet, so she scooted over on the sun-warmed concrete to make room for him.

"It's a crying shame, the way this place has fallen into ruin," he said, and sat, resting his elbows on his knees.

"It's what happens when no one is looking," she said quietly.

"The hives are empty—I guess the bees moved on to greener pastures, so to speak, after Granddad died."

"I didn't see any when I looked in the garage, either."

"The honey house."

"The what?"

"It's not a garage," he told her. "It's the honey house."

"The honey house," she repeated, and thought it a perfect name.

Luke raised a hand and rubbed the back of his neck. "I'd give my half-interest in hell to know who owns the place now."

Roxie thought for a second. "I know how you could find out."

"How?"

"Call the courthouse and ask them to check the property tax rolls."

He gave a decisive nod. "I'll do that first chance I get."

They fell silent then, basking in the warmth of the sun and the simple contentment of being together on such a beautiful day. Butterflies fluttered about on colorful wings while a pair of chipmunks played tag in and around the lilies. A bird in a nearby tree sang its heart out for them.

Roxie looked over at Luke and asked the question that had been in the back of her mind since the day she saw him step off the train. "What made you decide to come back to Blue Ridge? You've no family left here. Why didn't you start fresh somewhere else?"

"You know, you missed your calling in life," he drawled. "You ask questions like a prosecutor."

His teasing smile told her that he hadn't taken offense. "I just wondered. You might have had a better chance somewhere else, where people didn't know you and didn't care who your parents were or what you'd done."

Years of secreting his thoughts, of hiding his reactions, of never letting on, made it difficult at first. It seemed to him that the machinery governing his finer emotions had rusted from disuse. But he wanted to share with her as he'd never done with anyone else and, eventually, he cranked the machine and opened up more fully than he had ever done.

"It was partly pure old Bauer bullheadedness." A wry grin twisted his mouth, and he shook his head. "I never could do something easily if there was a harder way."

"Well, you certainly didn't pick an easy path, coming back," she said in a wry tone.

"True enough." Looking about him, he absorbed the simple beauty that surrounded them and felt a familiar sense of tranquility soothe him. "But family or not, Blue Ridge is my home. All those years behind bars, I kept dreaming of it. Building it up in my mind, I guess you'd say. Maybe even remembering things as being better than they really were."

He fell silent for a moment and then added almost as an afterthought, "And when you come right down to it, I really didn't have any place else to go."

"I've always wondered why people say they'd never live in a small town." She wasn't really asking a question, just thinking aloud.

He slid her a sideways glance. "Because everybody in a small town knows everybody else's business?"

"Which they do," she said, adding an eye roll for emphasis.

"Because nobody in a small town ever really forgets that you made a mistake?"

"Which they don't."

His stared into her eyes. "And yet you, like I, came back to Blue Ridge."

"Yes," she murmured. "Yes, I did."

It wasn't fair to expect disclosures from him without divulging anything of her own, but she didn't feel up to confessions at the moment. At the moment, she was fighting the urge to reach over and brush that errant lock of black hair off his brow. It was the craziest compulsion she'd ever had, and she wasn't quite sure how to deal with it.

To cover her agitation, she clasped her hands tightly together in her lap. "Are you glad you came back?"

"I used to dream about days like this," he said. "Of being wrapped in sunshine and silence, of wallowing in the smell of fresh air and ripening fruit, of walking where I wanted when I wanted, maybe even taking a dip in the pond out back of the orchard."

"You love this place."

"It's the only home I ever really had."

His tone was such a fusion of contentment and yearning that Roxie knew another piercing of her soul. What must it be like, to yearn for something as simple as being able to walk free? To dream of privacy the way most people dream of riches. The thought of it made her ache. The thought of Luke yearning and dreaming for such things made her ache with special poignancy.

"You make my old dreams sound mundane," she said with a tinge of sadness.

He sent a lazy smile in her direction. "And what exactly did you dream about?"

"Oh, all the usual things." Her shoulders bobbed in a brief, almost dismissive shrug. "A husband, a home, babies."

"Do you still dream of those things, Roxie?" he asked in a husky tone.

She raised her hand as if to cover her eyes from the sun, but actually she was hiding from the perceptive power of his gaze. "Oh, no, not these days."

His look said he didn't believe her.

"Honestly," she insisted. "Nowadays I dream of getting the warehouse's books to balance or of getting my desk cleared off, if even for only ten minutes."

His brows were pulled down into a deep V over his eyes. "Now that's what I can't make fit about you."

Her smile faltered slightly. "What?"

"Why aren't you married, with the home and the babies of your dreams? It doesn't make sense to me," he said almost to himself. "Don't the men around here have eyes in their heads? How have they let you get away?"

He seemed determined to press the point. She was equally determined not to discuss it. This had been such a lovely afternoon, and she didn't want thoughts of Arthur to spoil it.

"You make me sound like a prize bass," she complained. "Nobody let me get away because I'm not a catch. I'm a person, not a fish."

Though Roxie only meant to tease him, her words carried a stridency that caught Luke up short. The last thing he wanted to do was antagonize her for any reason. He should have known better than to pry; no one knew better than he how distressing unwanted prying could be. He thought perhaps it was time to end this idyllic spell before he once again said or did something to sever the slender thread of communication between them.

Standing, he stretched and said as easily as he could, "I know I was away from women for a long time, but believe me, it wasn't so long that I can't tell the difference between a woman and a fish."

Flushing, she too came to her feet. "Sorry."

His laughter was as warm and mellow as the buttery sunshine coating them. "No problem."

He stretched again. He was stalling, and he knew it. But each moment with her seemed so precious, so filled with the companionship he'd yearned for throughout all the long, lonely, lost years, he wanted to linger over every sweet second he spent with her. Especially here, with the freedom and the solitude he'd so craved in all the years of captivity. He felt as if he could stay here with her for all time and be happy. But in the end, he did what he had to do.

"I hate to say it, but I think it's time for us to go," he said with reluctance.

"I guess so," she said with equal reluctance.

Any hope that she would insist they stay longer was snuffed and he accepted the inevitable. Their idyll was over.

# CHAPTER 9

Walking behind Luke down the drive, Roxie tripped on a tree root. Turning, Luke saw her start to fall. Instinctively his arms shot out, and he lunged for her. She crashed against his chest, sending them both toppling with a heavy thud. Cradling her in his arms, he landed flat on his back, taking the full impact of their combined weight as he hit the packed dirt. They lay motionless, heartbeat to heartbeat, for a long moment.

Gradually, almost of its own volition, his hand came up. His fingertips grazed her cheek as he brushed the honey-blonde strands of her hair back off her face. Her skin was satin-smooth. Her breathing sent small puffs of air against his eyes, his mouth. Her lips were close enough to kiss.

"Are you hurt?" he asked, his heart thumping unsteadily.

Roxie knew she should get off him. But she was curiously loath to move a single muscle. Nestled against the length and warmth of his body, she could only look at him in utter wonderment as she felt all her inhibitions melting away.

The sunlight that filtered through the thick, leafy trees dappled over him, making him look romantic and handsome in the summer shade. His dark hair had curled a bit at the ends from the heat and humidity, and his gray eyes had gone as silver as a new dime. The smell of him, all hot and earthy, went straight to her head.

She shook her head fiercely, in both a delayed answer to his question and to deny the sensations rioting inside her. "No."

Her sigh tickled Luke's jaw. He sucked his breath in sharply, and her lowered lashes fluttered upward. Her eyes were a darker shade of blue than he'd ever seen them. Dark and liquid and shimmering like the finest silk. Shuddering, he fought against his surging need to kiss her, to touch her, to mold the soft contours of her body to the hard imprint of his own. Any other woman, and he swore he'd flip her onto her back and take her then and there. But this was Roxie, the one woman he could not have. And the only one he wanted.

He had long since learned the bitter lessons of self-control, but never had the lesson been so cruel. Never had he been so tempted to reject the constraints as he was now, totally captivated by her. But he knew how everyone else would view any relationship between them, knew she would be seen in a bad light by one and all, and he could not, he would not, subject her to such censure.

Through sheer force of will, he clamped his jaw tight and clenched his fists at his sides. That still didn't stop the white-hot need that roared unchecked inside him. He closed his eyes, trying to hide his turmoil even as the warm weight of her, the summery scent of her, the intimate flexure of her, continued to torment him.

With a feather-light touch, Roxie skimmed a fingertip along the scar on his cheek. She heard his ragged breath and watched his eyes fly open, saw them darken with want, burn with desire. Settled intimately atop him, she was fully aware of his arousal. And seeing his taut expression, feeling his tensed muscles, she was fully aware that he was resisting his feelings. She knew she should stop, knew it was wrong of her to continue tormenting him like this, but an intense need to explore the wonders of him, to know the splendor of his body beneath her hands, trampled her scruples and left them scattered in the dirt.

The pad of her finger came to rest against the corner of his mouth, and she felt the moist heat of his low groan. It was a sensual mouth, full, with a deeply masculine indentation. Giving in to temptation, she traced the curve of his top lip.

"Roxie," he said hoarsely.

She heard his warning but didn't heed it. Couldn't keep from gliding her finger on around, along that tempting bottom lip. She felt peculiarly detached from her actions, as if she'd stepped outside her body and was watching some other woman stroke him so provocatively.

Luke realized he needed to put an end to this. Now. She didn't know; she couldn't understand the shattering force of her effect. He opened his mouth to speak, and instead, turned his head a smidgen and gently closed his lips upon her finger, tasting the saltiness of her skin as he played his tongue against the tip. But in his mind his tongue sketched the puckered nipple of her breast, savoring the grainy texture.

Just the sight of her flesh imprisoned between his strong white teeth flustered Roxie no end. She wished she could think of a way to pull her finger out of his mouth without creating a fuss, but she was at a loss. At last he released her, and she pulled her hand back, feeling as though she had reached too close to a fire and hadn't realized it until the flames singed her.

Knowing he must set her away while he still could, Luke brought his hands up to do exactly that. His thumbs skimmed over the sides of her breasts and his grip tightened on her ribcage. Yet in his mind his palms filled with the pliant softness of those breasts, the buds firming to his persuasive caress.

He lay beneath her, full and aching, straining to curb his excitement, willing himself not to lift his hand higher, fighting the compulsion to trail his mouth up her arm to the slender column of her throat and beyond. Mentally he held her without restraint, his hands and lips seeking freely, feverishly, as their bodies twined together. The images pulsed through him with such consuming intensity that he feared he might do something he would forever regret.

With one motion, he rolled to his side and, making sure he didn't hurt her in the process, tumbled her to the ground. She lay there, immobile, gaping at him in wide-eyed shock. Ignoring her stunned expression, he bolted upright and dragged in slow, deep, steadying gulps of air.

Roxie sat up and shook her hair back. She had known he was aroused. She couldn't help but know, but her own arousal had obscured how very intensely he'd been stirred. All she had done was touch his cheek, his mouth. She would never have imagined such a painfully impassioned response. But his desire was obvious in his tense features, his still-trembling body. Heavy remorse burdened her for the way in which she had teased him.

"I'm sorry, Luke, I never meant—"

He held up a hand to cut her off. "Don't, Roxie, just don't."

"But—"

"It's over." He pushed to his feet. "Forget it."

He sounded so harsh, she felt even worse. "But I am sorry, Luke," she persisted in a papery voice. "I should never have—"

"You should have watched where you were walking," he interrupted. "You could have been hurt."

Her knees wobbling, she stood and swept what dirt she could from the back of her blouse and the legs of her slacks. She spoke in a hurried staccato that matched the agitation of her hands. "I'm so clumsy sometimes. I can't believe I—"

"Roxie," he said, and this time his voice was soothing, almost gentle.

She stood stock-still. Her body drummed with each agonizing beat of her heart as she slowly raised her gaze to meet his. The hint of a rueful smile indented his sensual mouth even as that silvered passion lingered in his eyes.

"It's all right, Roxie," he comforted her. "You couldn't know."

Never had she felt such a welling of emotion as she did now. It rose up inside her, so intense that she thought she would drown in the flood of guilt, relief, joy, and indefinable caring. She had to blink, hard, to keep it from pouring forth from her eyes.

"You couldn't help it," he went on, measuring each word carefully. "It wasn't anything you did. It was . . . it's been so long since . . . just being near"—he nearly said *you,* but managed to catch himself in time—"a woman . . . can excite me. It wasn't really you at all."

It was the biggest lie of all time. She was the only woman he'd ever really wanted, really wanted in such a soul-stirring way. But of course, he'd never be able to tell her that.

All her emotions drained away, leaving only an uncertain injured pique. Then she looked at him with a mixture of hurt and anger rigidly imprinted on her features. He recognized that harsh expression. Because he'd read rejection in too many faces not to know it when he saw it. A wall of glass broke in his chest as the last of his hope splintered into a million shards.

"I swear I won't touch you again," he said.

Irrationally, this irritated her further. Stiffening, she suggested they forget about it. "It's getting late," she said on a note that matched her bleak mien. "We'd best get going."

The shards pierced his soul as she spun on her heel and strode off down the drive. He wanted to tell her he hadn't meant that the way it sounded, that he was just trying to protect her from the slings and arrows of town gossip, but it was too late. Now he had no option but to follow her.

They walked down the shade-speckled drive in single file, silent, oblivious to the chattering of the squirrels, the whisper of the breeze through the trees, the checkered sunlight.

Luke suffered an agonizing inner upheaval. The time with Roxie was a memory to treasure, one to sustain him in his loneliness. But it was also a cruel reminder of all the wasted years, of all the years without someone special at his side, someone to share with, someone to shine a light against the darkness of his life.

He knew he was totally unacceptable for someone as sweet and good as Roxie. She was the unattainable one. The one forbidden and off-limits. Even beyond his far-reaching boundaries. That she had not only given him a second chance but had also shared her smile, her time and even her food with him had moved him beyond measure. He certainly didn't expect anything more. But having received those gifts from her, he didn't think he could bear going on with anything less.

He was well-acquainted with pain. He'd known all kinds of pain—that of desertion, of denial, of dehumanization. But he'd never before known the gut-wrenching pain of a loss like this. Without Roxie, without her smile to brighten his days, without her welcome company at lunch, his empty life would be more starkly barren than he could bear. Already the desolation shrouded his soul.

Roxie was thoroughly ashamed of herself for stirring Luke up like she had. On the other hand, she was distressed over being lumped together with all the other women who could excite him. The notion disturbed her in myriad ways. It depressed and annoyed her. It bruised her ego, offended her sensibilities. She didn't want to be *a* woman who affected him so strongly. She wanted to be the *only* woman.

Her step faltered as they approached the road. Good brown gravy, what was she thinking? She swiftly regained her balance, thankful that Luke was still walking behind her and couldn't see her expression. A ringing box on the ears could not have stunned her more. The unexpected revelation was all the more astounding for its veracity.

Still lost in thought, she resumed her seat in the sidecar while he climbed onto the motorcycle. Covertly, she watched the tightening of muscles beneath the legs of his blue jeans as he braced his left foot on the ground for balance and used his right to start the engine. Then she turned her eyes resolutely away, resisting the urge to study him and mulling over her startling realization.

She didn't waste time doubting the truth of it. It was obvious in the sudden dancing of her nerves, the catch in her breath, the tightening of her tummy whenever he was near. She had always been attracted to him, she realized, and now that she'd come to know him, to like and respect him, she was certain it would be all too easy to feel a great deal more for him. But still she shied away from letting herself feel that something more. Love meant opening yourself up to another, to making yourself vulnerable to the searing pain of disillusionment. She had vowed never to be so vulnerable again. Was she possibly ready now to take the risk? Was she ready to take a chance on her tumultuous feelings for Luke? She didn't know. She just didn't know if she could again endure the type of emotional devastation Arthur had put her through.

One thing she did know, however, was that she owed Luke an apology. She had behaved badly, teasing and tempting him with no thought for how it might affect him. Then she'd compounded her guilt by venting her vexation at him when all he'd done was to try to make her feel better about it. Her selfish behavior had spoiled the perfection of their afternoon together and though no amount of apologies could restore it, she had to let him know how very sorry she was.

As soon as they pulled up in front of her house, Roxie clambered out of the sidecar. She waited on the sidewalk until Luke had killed the motorcycle engine and dismounted. Then she wet her dry lips with a nervously flicking tongue and opened her mouth.

A stamping of feet interrupted her before she could speak. She whirled to see Bill and Frederick and John rushing out of the house and down the porch steps toward where they were standing. She sensed Luke's immediate defensive stance and prayed this day would not get any worse.

"What's going on here?" Bill demanded, a belligerent scowl darkening his rounded face.

Obviously, her prayer had gone unanswered. With as calm a manner as she could muster under the circumstances, which, with three brothers glowering fiercely at her head-on and one Bauer radiating hostile strength at her back, weren't too serene, she said, "Why, Bill, what can you mean?"

"What are you doing here with *him?*" Bill's jaw thrust pugnaciously forward, he glared at Luke.

Roxie peered over her shoulder and nearly shuddered. It was worse than she'd feared. Luke stood with his feet planted apart, his head cocked slightly as he sent her brother a look that would wither a plant to its roots. A tacit challenge was boldly clear in his stance, his attitude. This was the old Luke, and she wasn't at all sure she wanted to have anything to do with him. From the militant noise that Bill was making, however, it was all too clear *he* would thoroughly enjoy having something to do with Luke.

Ignoring Frederick, whose mustache was bristling with indignation, she sent a silent appeal to her youngest brother. But John, usually the most temperate of the three, mirrored Bill's readiness for a fight. Her heart sinking, she said on a resigned sigh, "We went for a ride."

"A ride!" Bill echoed, furious.

"On *that?*" Frederick pointed an accusatory finger at the motorcycle.

"With *him?*" John shouted.

She stiffened. They made it sound as if she'd have done better to go riding with John Dillinger! Coldly, she asked, "Is there

152

a problem?"

Brushing off her question, Bill faced Luke and issued a terse order. "Stay away from my sister, Bauer."

Luke would have liked nothing better than to release some of his pent-up pain and frustration in a fight. For one fleeting fraction of a second he nearly listened to his pumping adrenaline and let his fists fly. But he hadn't spent the last two months trying to turn his life around only to throw it all away in one angry moment. He kept his mouth shut and his fists at his sides.

"She doesn't need the likes of you bothering her," Bill spouted.

"Absolutely not," Frederick put in.

"Leave her alone, Bauer." John repeated Bill's earlier order.

"Honestly, you three, I'm not a child!" Roxie burst out. It was clearly evident that her brothers intended to provoke a fight, and she was now utterly furious with them. A slight breeze teased her wind-tousled hair, and she pushed it out of her face. "I'm perfectly capable of deciding with whom I wish to ride."

Throwing her a frown of pure disgust, Bill muttered, "That's debatable."

Roxie stood there as if she was frozen in place. She wanted Luke to leave before a fight truly did erupt. She didn't doubt for a second that he could hold his own against her brothers. John made his living doing farm chores and was in pretty good physical shape, but the same couldn't be said of her other two brothers. Bill was pudgy in the belly and Frederick was soft in the hands. Luke could probably take them on, separately or together, and come out the winner. But he might hurt one of them. And she couldn't have borne it if she was the cause of him having to go back to prison.

Turning to him now, she said with warm sincerity, "I'm sorry you've been subjected to this rude display of bad manners, Luke. I assure you that my brothers, all three of them, generally show more courtesy, if not more sense."

Alert to her every nuance of expression, he could read the storm still raging in her eyes and his admiration for her control gave him the impetus to respond in kind. "That's all right, Roxie. It's understandable, given the circumstances. I believe it would be best if I left—"

"You're darn right it would be best!" Bill interjected.

Roxie flashed him a deadly look before presenting Luke with her prettiest smile, the one Arthur had always called dazzling. "I don't blame you for wanting to get away, but you won't forget that we're going to the carnival tonight, will you? I promise you, I'll be there at six-thirty."

He understood her motivation. She'd been goaded into this by her brothers. But he was quick to grasp at the chance she offered him to rectify all the transgressions of the afternoon. Besides, in the brilliancy of that smile, he'd have agreed to anything.

"I won't forget," he said without the least hesitation. "Meet you at the entrance to the fairgrounds, right?"

"Right," she verified in a voice rife with enthusiasm. "They won't turn on the Ferris wheel lights until dark, so that will give us time to fill up on roasted peanuts and barbecued chicken and maybe even some cotton candy before we ride it."

A glint of amusement entered his silvery eyes. "Sounds like a recipe for an upset stomach."

"Oh, what's a little dyspepsia between friends?" she said with a dismissive wave of her hand.

They laughed together, and it felt as right as right could be.

Explosive little squawks of shock sparked between her brothers, igniting Bill to fire a shrill "Are you crazy?" at her.

"Are you sure you don't want me to pick you up?" Roxie asked Luke, still paying no attention to her brothers.

"It's close enough to the boardinghouse I can walk," he answered.

"I'll see you at six-thirty then."

He turned away and then back, looking rugged and handsome, windblown and sunbaked, disreputable and dangerous. "You'll be okay?"

"I can handle them," she assured him.

A smile, soft and knowing and heartening, passed between them. For Luke, it brought renewed hope. For Roxie, it brought another jumbling of her already disordered emotions.

With a fervent gratitude to the antagonistic brothers who had inadvertently given him another chance, Luke climbed onto the motorcycle, revved the engine and rode away, his sleeves riffling in the wind. Roxie followed him with hungry eyes, her vision clouded by the memory of his strong arms holding her above him, his hard body pinned beneath hers.

But the instant he rounded the corner her vision cleared, and she pulled herself back to the present. Bill and Frederick and John clamored at her, demanding to know if she'd lost her mind, her sense, her morals. Finally, she felt she had to speak or be smothered in the avalanche of their accusations.

"I can't imagine what my morals have to do with it," she said in a restrained tone. "We're going on a date, not a heist."

Bill clenched his fists. "How can you make jokes about this?"

Maybe her mother was right, Roxie thought. Maybe the hospital *had* made a mistake. What other explanation could there be for a brother like Bill? She sighed audibly. "I joke because if I didn't lighten my mood a bit, I'd be seriously tempted to run you through with Dad's sharpest carving knife."

"You're not going out with that jailbird," Frederick said with a snarl.

"What right have you got to interfere in my life?" she snapped. "What right have you got to insult my guests?"

"We didn't mean to be rude, Roxie." John's face didn't bear any of his normal cheer. From his brown eyes to his down-turned mouth, he looked worried. "But it was such a shock, seeing you with Bauer that we just sort of blew up."

She gave him the gimlet eye. "I still don't see that it's any of your business."

"We care about you, Roxie," Bill said, almost irritably. "And we're concerned about you."

"If we interfere," Frederick added, "it's only for your own good."

She covered her face with her hands. She was no longer certain whether she was infuriated, amused, or both. It seemed no matter where she went or what she did, she couldn't escape people's misguided but sincere desire to protect her from herself. It was a conspiracy of concern that was driving her crazy.

Amusement won out. She dropped her hands, raised her eyes heavenward, and intoned gravely, "Dear Lord, please save me from all these fools who wish to run my life for my own good."

"Okay, okay, make jokes about it," Bill sputtered. "Why should we waste our time worrying if you don't."

"My point precisely," Roxie said in a no-nonsense tone. "Now, if you'll excuse me, I've got a date to get ready for. And if I'm not mistaken, you three have perfectly lovely wives waiting for you at home."

She darted away before they could find new ammunition to fire at her. Glancing back, she saw them, their heads shaking as they stood on the sidewalk conferring together—more than likely, she thought, on whether a straight jacket or a net would be more effective to use on her. She dashed up the porch steps and into the house, running to the pounding beat of her heart. Each step rang with the message that pursued her.

She was going out with Luke on a real date!

"Roxie?" Mary called from the kitchen.

She did an about-face at the foot of the stairs and headed to the back of the house, coming to a stop in the kitchen doorway. "What, Mother?"

Mary looked over at Roxie, not missing a stroke of her paring knife on the potato she was peeling. "Are you okay, dear?"

"Yes. Why?"

"You look a little harried."

"I'm fine. Really. But I am in a hurry."

Mary paused then and pointed with the blade of her knife toward the jar of honey that she'd moved from the table to the counter. In a tone utterly without inflection, she said, "Did Luke bring the honey?"

A tingle tracked up Roxie's spine at the deliberate lack of expression. "Yes, he did. It was one of three jars he inherited from his grandfather. He said it was to thank me for the lunches I brought him."

Mary resumed her interest in her potato, turning her back to her daughter. "Do you think he'd mind if I used a little of it the next time I fry chicken?"

"Oh, no, I'm sure he wouldn't mind a bit."

"Especially if you invited him to dinner."

Roxie glanced at her mother's slim back, her slenderness emphasized by the apron tied around her waist, and knew another burst of gratitude. "Speaking of which," she said with studied nonchalance, "I won't be home for dinner tonight."

Mary raised her head to look across the room at her daughter. "Oh?"

"I have a date to go to the carnival." After a thudding heartbeat, she added, "With Luke."

"Oh," her mother said again. Then she smiled before returning her attention to the potato.

It was enough. Encouraged by her mother's attitude, Roxie

tore upstairs to get ready. Her brothers' animosity was forgotten, and her own lingering guilt over her actions this afternoon faded into naught.

Her bedroom looked much as it had when she was a girl. She remembered coming home from school one day and finding that her mother had decorated it fit for a princess. Even though the pink walls and white eyelet curtains and lampshade were too juvenile and frilly for her now, she had more important things on her mind than redoing her room—especially tonight.

After taking a long soak in the bathtub and washing and pin-curling her hair, she put on her cotton wrapper and went rooting in her closet for something to wear. She tried on three different dresses but rejected one of them as too long, one as too short, and one as too dowdy before finally settling on a pale blue voile dress that she had been saving for a special occasion. She wanted to look pretty for Luke. What she didn't want was a repeat of this afternoon's performance.

She glanced at her bedside clock and saw that it was already fifteen minutes till six. Time was getting away from her and she was nowhere near ready. She checked to see if her hair was dry. It was, so she pulled out the bobby pins, tossed them into the top drawer of her vanity, then sat down on the tufted bench to finish up.

As she made to pick up her hairbrush, she caught sight of herself in the mirror. Leaving the brush laying on the vanity, she reached out to trace the shape of her face with her fingers and remembered how she'd traced the line of the scar on Luke's cheek. She remembered his shuddering breath, his rampaging heartbeat, his undeniable arousal. All from a single touch.

But he'd said he would react the same with any woman.

She flattened her hand on the cool glass and imagined the heat of his skin kissing her flesh. The memory of his warmth pulsated through her. With such delicate deliberation she had

158

touched him, savoring each inch of the firm bone and textured skin. With equal deliberation she had separated herself from what she now recognized as a poor attempt at seduction. And his body had pulsed from the force of it.

He'd said it wasn't anything she'd done.

Dropping her hand into her lap, she tipped her head back and closed her eyes, thinking she made a lousy vamp and wondering if she would ever know the warmth of his embrace, the heat of his kiss.

He'd sworn not to touch her again.

Roxie's eyes flew open as yet another revelation came clear to her. "Oh, Luke," she whispered to her reflection, "I want you to touch me again. I don't want it to be the same with just any woman. I want it to be special with me. I don't want you to admire me, Luke. I want you to love me."

She wanted it as surely as she breathed. She wanted it because, ready for the risk or not, she loved him. She loved Luke Bauer.

# CHAPTER 10

Calliope music hooted over the town, competing with the voices of carnival barkers hocking their wares. The Ferris wheel topped the trees and the town's water tower, the mouthwatering aromas of hot dogs and barbecue and freshly-roasted peanuts filled the air, and the Bearded Lady and a two-headed calf vied for the dubious honor of strangest attraction. In the nearby field Model T's and Packards sat bumper to rump with the tied-up horses and mules that had hauled in buckboards of farmers' families who were desperate to forget, if only for a little while, the Depression and the drought.

A steady stream of carnival-goers flowed toward the arched gate of the fairgrounds. Beside the ticket booth just outside that gate, Luke stood with his hands in his pockets watching the people hurry by. It reminded him of when he was a boy with no parents to take him on the rides and no money to go on his own. He'd snuck onto the carousel once, when he was eight, but he'd been caught before the ride started. The motorman running it had grabbed him by his dirty shirt collar and holey seat pants and, in front of God and all the sneering, jeering customers who'd paid their admission, had thrown him off. He hadn't been to the carnival since.

Things hadn't changed all that much, he realized as he watched the parade of people. He was aware of each side-long look, each inimical whisper, and each hurried footstep going past him. There was a time when he'd have met the look with an arrogant curl of his lip, interrupted the whisper with an insolent suggestion that the speakers take a flying leap, or stepped brazenly in front of those scurrying to get out of his way, issuing a challenge that didn't need words.

But that was long ago, another lifetime, another man. Now he did his best to fade into the woodwork of the booth, to suppress the deep desire to respond as he always had, with anger and arrogance and a pretense that he didn't give a damn. He did his best to ignore the hurt.

Easier said than done. Because each time he caught another contemptuous glance cast his way, he thought of Roxie. He didn't think he could restrain himself if anyone looked at her that way. And they would. He knew they would. If she were with him, she'd become part of the target. His reputation would rub off on her. Worse, because she was with him, he'd have no choice. He would have to restrain himself.

He jammed his fists deeper into the pockets of his clean khaki pants and stared down at the dirt. He'd told her he had come back to Blue Ridge because he had nowhere else to go. But in truth it was pride that had compelled him to return to home. This was the place he had to prove himself. These were the people he had to show he had changed. But even knowing how tough it would be didn't make it any easier to deal with the constant condemnation. Some days it was easy to rein in the hurt and resentment. To turn the other cheek, so to speak. Other days it was harder. He felt as if he were being continually tested but never received a grade.

The squeal of girlish giggles arrested his musing. He looked up before he could stop himself. A trio of teenagers bedecked in their Saturday night finest gawked back, then bent their heads together for a conclave of zealous chattering. An unfriendly breeze carried the taunting hiss of the words he most hated:

161

prison, con, crook. Within his pockets his fists balled even tighter.

And he knew with certainty that he could not subject Roxie to this.

Pivoting on his heel, he strode at a clip guaranteed to get him as far away as possible before she turned up. She probably wouldn't show up anyway. It was already a quarter till seven. She hadn't really wanted to go to the carnival with him. She'd been spurred into it by her brothers.

He stepped into the street, intending to hightail it back to the boardinghouse. A horn blared, brakes shrieked, and an old black automobile swerved directly into his path. He lurched to a stop. Automatically every muscle tensed as he went on alert, poised for trouble. He felt his eyes narrow when he looked down.

Roxie's wavy hair tossed in the breeze as she poked her head out the window to frown up at him. "Where are you going? The carnival is the other way!"

"I know," he said tersely.

"Is it because I'm late?" She smiled crookedly, contritely. "I'm sorry, but time just got away from me. And parking is at a premium here tonight, so I was—"

An angry horn and an impatient shout interrupted her flowing explanation. She glanced at the old Dodge idling roughly behind her, then gestured at Luke. "Get in and we'll talk while I try to find a place to park in the field."

Another imperious trumpeting terminated his hesitation. He darted around to the passenger side, and even before he shut the door they were moving. The car smelled of her rosewater fragrance and the deep summer air. He closed his eyes and let his relief seep into every pore. She had come. He only now realized how much he'd longed she would.

"As I was saying before we were so rudely interrupted, I'm sorry I was late." Roxie stole a peek at him, wondering if she dare confess that it was because she'd spent so much time trying to decide what to wear. "But I wasn't really all that late. Why were you leaving?"

Luke straightened, then looked at her. For a moment he couldn't breathe, much less speak. She wore a dress unlike any he'd seen on her at work—a soft, summery sort of dress in a light blue color with short sleeves and a scalloped neckline. The skirt was full yet clingy, hugging the shape of her thighs as he himself longed to do. Somehow he forced himself to look away.

"I realized," he said in a monotone, "that it would be best if we forgot the whole thing."

"Forgot it?" she said as she banged across the field, the frame of the car squawking in protest whenever she hit a rut. "Why?"

"You don't have to go through with this, Roxie. I know you suggested we go to the carnival in order to goad your brothers. That's why I went along with it. I didn't really expect you to show up, and when you were late, well—"

"I do not consider a measly fifteen minutes late," she broke in, her voice frosty.

Before he could respond, she swung into an empty parking spot and jerked to a halt. She faced him and for the first time he saw a faint resemblance between Roxie and her fractious brother Bill. Not in the shape of her face so much as in the way she thrust up her chin and met his gaze head on.

"Whatever the reason," she said, "we agreed to go to the carnival tonight. I was glad about it. Obviously you're not. I'd like to know why. Is it because you're ashamed to be seen with me?"

"How could you even suggest—"

"What else am I to believe? That you think I'll be ashamed of being seen with you? That says a lot about what you think of me, doesn't it?"

Luke shook his head, wondering how best to explain it. "You

don't understand how they'll look at you, Roxie, how they'll talk. I don't want to subject you to that."

She stared at him for a very long time. Long enough for him to notice that she had darkened her fair lashes and daubed on a pretty color of pink lipstick. Long enough for him to realize that she had taken the trouble to look her best tonight. Long enough to wonder why.

At length she sighed, a drawn-out expulsion that reeked of disappointment. "You know, I would never have figured you to be the sort to run away."

A face full of ice water would have been less effective. After a startled second in which he gaped, dumbfounded, Luke closed his mouth with a snap and ejected himself from the car. Roxie didn't move until he'd yanked open her door. Then she slid out with a knowingly triumphant smile.

The distance to the ticket booth was covered in bustling silence.

Luke's anger with her scarcely lasted beyond the first step. He knew she was right. He couldn't run away. Wasn't that why he'd come back to Blue Ridge in the first place? But he didn't feel he could speak or slow down or he'd lose the courage to go through that entrance gate.

Worried on his behalf more than her own, Roxie kept silent and kept pace. For his sake, for their sake, she hoped she had done the right thing by pushing him into doing this. Otherwise—

"How many tickets do you need?" the man in the booth asked.

Roxie looked at Luke.

He shrugged and said "You're the one who wants to ride the Ferris wheel."

"It's a nickel a ride," the ticket seller said helpfully.

"Let's buy two each," she decided, digging for some change in the bottom of her purse.

"Put your money away," Luke instructed her. "I'm paying."

Just inside the gate, the babble of voices fell for several stunned seconds, then rose with renewed vigor. They walked a gauntlet of stares down carnival row, passing the guess-your-weight barker, the peep show, and other crowd-pullers on their way to the food booths. There, they perused rows of steamed, grilled, boiled, barbecued and baked delights to fill their every craving.

A tight ball of anger wound within Luke's stomach, twisting more tightly with each disapproving look cast their way, each derogatory whisper he heard. He couldn't tolerate exposing Roxie to the barbs he routinely received. As soon as they reached the hot dog booth he said flatly, "I don't think this was such a good idea."

Roxie took one look at his taut jaw and decided he was right. But they were here, and she wasn't a quitter. "I think it's a great idea. I'm dying for a hot dog."

"I'm not really hungry," he said.

"My mouth's been watering all evening."

"I think we should go."

"We're already here, and I'm hungry even if you're not. Besides, it's my treat."

He frowned and said, "No, it's not your treat. We're on a date. I'm paying."

"As you pointed out earlier," she reminded him, "it's not a real date. I put you on the spot, pressing you into this just to annoy Bill and Frederick and John. Therefore, I should pay."

"No, you shouldn't," he said. "You're not."

She gave him a look that reminded him of her mother.

"I should, and I am," Roxie said. "Or, at least," she amended hastily, taking in his glowering disapproval, "I'm paying half. We'll go Dutch. How's that?"

He didn't like it and told her so, but when she held out he finally agreed to it.

"If you don't like Dutch treats," she said with a wicked grin, "you'll just have to ask me out properly next time."

"I'll do that," Luke said, his whole being cheered with the thought of there being a next time.

They ordered hot dog sandwiches nestled in newspaper boats, a bottle of orange pop for her and a glass of cold spring water for him. Then they found seats across from each other at one of the picnic tables that had been set up and talked about work as they ate. Luke began to relax. It was part of what made Roxie so special, this ability to loosen the coil of tension within him.

Roxie, in turn, felt her spirit lighten as she sensed his mood mellowing. It was part of her newly discovered love, this finding joy in his joy. Immersed as they were in each other, she didn't realize someone had approached.

"Um, hello, Roxie," Louise Spencer said with nervous hesitation.

"Hello, Louise." She smiled up at the Ladies Aide member. "You know Luke Bauer, don't you?"

Carefully avoiding looking in his direction, Louise waved her hand toward the table where her husband sat. "Uh, well, anyway, Harry and I just wondered if everything is okay."

Roxie stiffened. She glanced at all two hundred and fifty pounds of Harry Spencer with his beady eyes shining almost malevolently in his red face. She gave him a tight smile, then transferred it to Louise. "Well, the hot dogs are hot and the orange pop is cold."

Louise had the grace to blush. She murmured a quick, "I'll see you at the next meeting," and scurried back to her table.

Seeing the grim set of Luke's face, Roxie rather wished she'd told Louise what she thought of her and had booted her on her ample rump to emphasize the point. Instead, she said too cheerily, "My hot dog is really good. How's yours?"

"You're going to lose friends over this, Roxie," he predicted.

"Don't worry about me, Luke. I'm perfectly capable of handling a few snubs."

"You don't know how vindictive people can be. You're so good, you don't expect the worst from others, but—"

"But if you keep this up, you'll see the worst from me," she broke in, only half-teasing. "You don't need to protect me. Not only do I feel that I'm capable enough on my own, I assure you I get more than enough over-protection from my family."

She could see she hadn't convinced him. Frustrated, still annoyed with Louise's well-meaning but aggravating interruption, she bit down hard on her hot dog. A squirt of bright yellow mustard spurted out the end of her bun and across the table, splattering the front of his bone-white shirt. For a second she stared at the stain in horror. Then, not knowing what else to do, she took out her handkerchief out of her purse, dipped it in his water and reached over to dab at it.

"I'm so sorry, Luke! I should have been more careful!"

He stayed her agitated hand. As much as he'd have enjoyed her ministrations—he'd always longed for someone to fuss over him in all the little, tender ways—he didn't want to toss any more fuel into the speculative fire he could see on the faces of those around them. He pried the handkerchief from her grip and dampened the spot on his shirt.

"Now this would be a prime example of what one of my old cellmates always called the boomerang effect," he remarked with a solemn frown.

"Boomerang effect?"

"Anger always comes back at you," he explained.

"Because I was furious with that woman for spoiling our evening," she guessed, her mood lightening when his frown turned up into a crooked smile.

The words rushed to the tip of her tongue. She longed to say them, longed to tell him she loved him. But she had to be content with saying, "She hasn't spoiled our evening. It would take a lot more than that to spoil it. At least for me."

Luke looked at her and all the stares blurred, all the whispers muted. So long as she smiled at him like that, with such tender caring, he couldn't see or hear anything else. He wanted to tell her how much her smile meant to him, how much *she* meant to him. But he still had difficulty expressing his gentler feelings, even with her. It seemed impossible for him to find a way to say what he felt so deeply.

She saved him the trouble of finding those words when she asked, "Are you ready for some cotton candy?"

He grimaced as he passed her handkerchief back. "You're really going to eat that stuff?"

"What's the point in coming to the carnival if you don't indulge in some spun sugar?" she said on a laugh.

"Have at it," he said and stood.

Roxie threw away their trash while Luke returned his pop bottle for the penny deposit. As they walked away from the table, she quite deliberately set her hand on his arm. She left it there as they walked down the midway in the lowering dusk.

"I'm beginning to believe," he drawled, "that there's a real streak of rebellion in you, after all."

She laughed. "I told you so."

They strolled slowly, *ooh*ing when the strongman lifted a draft horse clean over his head, *aah*ing at the beautiful handmade raffle quilts hanging in the back of one of the booths, and completely ignoring the dour-faced night riders who were trying to recruit new members. Every so often they would look over and smile at each other. Words would have been superfluous.

After Roxie had satisfied her sweet tooth with a fluffy mound of spun sugar candy and Luke had crunched down a small bag's worth of caramel corn, they got in line to ride the Ferris wheel.

The sun went down and the carnival lights came on as their swinging metal car whisked them up, up, up until familiar landmarks looked small and the people on the ground became doll-like.

"Isn't this swell?" Roxie laughed with delight, her stomach dropping toward her toes as their gondola swooped downward toward earth again.

Luke was sitting with his arm slung along the back of their car. He wasn't quite embracing her slender shoulders. Almost, but not quite. He watched the breeze lift her hair about her shining face and her skirt billow about her slender legs, and he couldn't have agreed more.

"Yeah," he said, shooting her one of his infrequent grins. "Swell."

The second time they rode the Ferris wheel, it stopped with them at the top while the man at the control stick let some new people get on. Roxie thought it was both scary and sublime, rocking over the crowd and the fairgrounds as if floating on air. Dust swirled up from the ground and voices echoed hollowly on the evening breeze.

"Be careful," she cautioned Luke when he leaned forward in the swaying bucket for a better view.

His grin widened as he glanced over his shoulder at her. "Are you saying you won't grab me if I start to fall?"

She wondered what he would say if she told him that she had already fallen. Fallen in love with him, that is. Before she could speculate about it too much, the motorman started the wheel revolving again and they swept down and then back up at a spine-tingling speed that had her gasping for breath and Luke laughing with the glee that she suspected he'd never experienced as a child.

"Are you ready to go?" he asked her when they finally got off the Ferris wheel.

She'd hoped to ride one of the carousel's painted ponies, maybe even try to win some useless prize at one of the booths, but she realized that he'd probably had enough for one evening and simply said, "I'm ready when you are."

Figuring they were safe from prying eyes, Luke slipped an arm around Roxie's waist as they walked through the field to her car. Her skirt rustled softly, femininely about her calves, and he imagined the gentle hush of it beneath his palm. Her hair whisked in the playful breeze, and he pictured the honey-gold of it threaded about his fingers. Her fragrance wafted on the air, and he could almost taste the sweetness of it upon his lips as he pressed his mouth against the pulse of her throat.

"It's a nice evening," he said, when they reached her car.

Roxie thought it was a beautiful evening, but she simply stopped beside the driver's door and murmured, "Yes, it is."

"Not the least bit muggy."

"No, not at all."

He squinted up at the old gold orb climbing the night sky. "Full moon tonight."

She leaned back against her car and clutched the strap of her purse with both hands. "It sure is bright."

They were stalling, making small talk, because they were reluctant to say good-night.

"Are you going home from here?" he asked her after a few more inane observations.

She shrugged, wondering where this was leading. "Where else would I go?"

"Out to the old schoolhouse."

"The old schoolhouse?"

"It's the perfect place to watch the stars come out."

"Ah."

"You interested?"

"Absolutely." She wouldn't have admitted it to save her soul, but she hoped he had more in mind than seeing stars. "Would you like to drive?"

He would and, after opening the passenger door for her, he did.

They headed out of town, the headlights bouncing off row-crops shriveling in the fields and pens empty of cattle or pigs as they rattled over yet another country washboard of a road. Finally they came to a small grove of trees that ringed a weathered wooden cube of a building with boarded-up windows and an X made of two-by-four's barring the door. An old merry-go-round missing a couple of seats sat in the middle of the dirt yard, a black iron bell hung silently from a hook on the porch overhang, and a narrow outhouse leaned lopsidedly at a discreet distance in the back.

Roxie laughed as she looked around. "I'd forgotten all about this place."

"I rediscovered it on my walks." Luke didn't say that he'd gone looking for it. In the long-ago days it had been his place of solace. He'd broken into the building more times than he could count, simply to sit in the cool dark solitude.

"My brothers went to grade school here."

"I did, too."

She made a moue. "I looked forward to coming here as well, but it closed the year before I started school. It took me months to get over my disappointment."

"It used to be where I brought girls to pitch a little woo," he said with a rakish grin.

She lowered her lashes and peered at him from beneath them. "Used to be, you say?"

He couldn't believe she could be flirting with him. The mere thought of it accelerated his heartbeat. He thrust open his door.

"Let's go sit out in the breeze."

Roxie watched him cut around the front of the car, his white shirt showing up starkly against the blackness, then stepped out when he opened her door. She left her purse on the front seat and followed him. Leaves rustled in the trees, night birds chirped, and locusts whirred in a cacophonous harmony as he led her up three steps to the wooden porch. For the second time that day, they sat side by side. Only this time they deliberately sat close to each other.

She felt a gentle puff of wind cooling her skin. Unreasonably, her blood began warming. Luke was so close, so achingly close. A stretch of her finger and she would know how the night air sat upon his arm.

She peeked sidelong at him. "So did you?" she asked, and heard the huskiness in her voice.

"Did I what?" Luke felt his body respond to every sound and every move she made, but there wasn't anything he could do about it.

"Pitch a little woo. You know, with all those girls you said you brought here."

"My God, the questions you ask."

She aimlessly twirled a strand of hair around her finger. "You had quite a reputation back then, you know."

"I did?"

"Luke Bauer, the lady-killer," she confirmed. "The girls in my high school class were always gossiping about you."

"Now, why doesn't that surprise me?" he said with a twisted smile.

"It was all very complimentary, I assure you."

"How so?"

"Speculation about your . . . prowess . . . was rampant. And when Kay Ray Kelly turned up pregnant, we—"

Roxie stopped cold. What in tarnation was she saying? She

chanced a look at Luke. He was staring at the toe of his shoe, his face the expressionless mask she so hated. Thinking she should have her mouth taped permanently shut, she finished on a shaky whisper, "But of course it wasn't you."

Moonglow glossed his dark hair as he shook his head. "The last thing I would ever do is bring another unwanted child into the world."

Sorrow spun a web within her soul. She wished she could tell him she was sorry, that she hadn't meant to be so insensitive, but she somehow knew an apology would simply make things worse. The past held such a grip on the present, at times it seemed to her to be a deathlock.

Luke understood Roxie's disquiet and the reason for it. The need to comfort her overrode any dejection he himself felt whenever he thought of his past. He leaned back on his elbows, crossed an ankle over his bent knee, and said with lazy intimation, "As far as I can recall, I never heard a word about you from any of the boys. You were obviously one of the saintly girls who held out for marriage."

A searching look told her he wasn't simply trying to be valiant. He appeared very much at ease. A bit of her own tension diminished. "With a family like mine, I had little choice," she said lightly. "You've seen how protective my brothers can be. When I was a teenager I felt positively smothered."

"You bring a lot of it on yourself," he said.

"How?"

"You just have that way about you. You look as if you need protecting, need someone to look out for you." Luke refrained from suggesting that he be that someone.

Tension rebounded, redoubled in force. Roxie gazed up at the milky band of stars that now stretched across the black sky and wondered whether she could tell him. The decision was pre-ordained. If she wanted any sort of real relationship with him, she had to expose her vulnerabilities. She had to risk the hurt and disappointment to gain the joyful contentment that only being loved by the one you love can bring.

"I think maybe you're right," she said at last. "Even when I went to college, people always seemed to watch out for me. But then, it was a small women's college, the kind where you know everyone on campus and they all know you. Sometimes I felt like I was still in high school."

Luke could sense the buildup to something important. Willing himself to sound casual, he remarked, "You said you worked in St. Louis after college."

"Yes, I kept books for a dress manufacturer." This was her moment, but Roxie wasn't at all certain how to proceed. In the end, she tossed her hurt out with a saucy, "That's where I fell from sainthood."

He said nothing, for which she was grateful. Having made the plunge, she decided to go ahead and swim. "He was my boss. And he was everything all the boys back home had never been—cosmopolitan, sophisticated, cultured. I tumbled completely." She grimaced. "A bad choice of words but highly accurate. Because the company forbade involvement between employees, all our meetings were clandestine, hurried. It was only after I was well and truly involved that I learned he was married. And not to just any woman, but to the daughter of the company's owner."

It cost him no little effort, but Luke managed not to spit out the crude descriptives with which he was castigating the man who'd hurt her so.

"Of course I instantly broke it off." She laughed, a sour little laugh that left a bad taste in her mouth. "But my attack of scruples didn't last long. When he swore to me that he would leave his wife for me, that we would be married as soon as his divorce was final, it all started up again—the meetings, the rushed gropings. I hated myself. But I loved him, or thought I did. So I continued to see him."

She hung her head. Her hair shimmered golden in the darkness. Luke longed to brush it back with a soothing hand, to comfort her within his embrace. But, of course, he did neither of those things.

"It went on for almost another year," she continued in a voice so low it was difficult to hear. "He kept telling me that he was going to leave his wife just as soon as he'd saved enough money for us to live on, that he and his wife had separate bedrooms, that he'd hardly touched her since we met."

Roxie drew a breath that burned her lungs. "Then one day his wife came to his office. She was a pretty thing, petite, well-dressed. And she was obviously, heavily pregnant. I felt sick, shamed, and hurt. I wasn't able to cope, so I quit my job and I came home."

It took all her courage, but she raised her eyes to his. "Oh, Luke, don't you see? I let it go on for almost a full year after I knew he was married. How can you possibly think I'm good or sweet? Now you must think I'm little better than a—"

Luke shushed her in the swiftest, most effective way he knew. He wrapped his arms around her, lowered his head, and silenced her with a kiss.

# Chapter 11

Gentle, undemanding, a gift of solace, Luke's kiss calmed Roxie. She relaxed within his embrace, giving herself over to him completely, taking comfort in the strength of him. Her palm pressed against his chest and her own heart echoed the erratic rhythm of his. She sighed, and her lips parted for him.

For a single heartbeat they were immobile. Time, the world, even their breaths, hung suspended in that one unending moment. Then, with a low, anguished moan, Luke's mouth came down on hers and his tongue gained entry with a kiss that was fierce and hot and demanding.

Without so much as a token of resistance, Roxie surrendered to his demand. Her body melted against his, so warm it burned right through the thin material of her dress. Her hands wound into his hair, so soft it whispered through her fingers. She was filled with his scent, so musky and male. Her whole being was absorbed by him, enthralled, enchanted, enraptured by his kiss.

Years of restraint gave way to a tumult of passion. Wanting grew inside Luke, a huge and hungry thing as he whisked his hands over her, down the supple line of her back to the nip of her waist, the curve of her hips, and then up her sides. He'd fantasized about holding her, caressing her, but no fantasy had ever produced the dewy softness of her skin, the fragrant silk of her hair, the delicate rise and fall of her breasts with each breath she drew. She responded to his every touch with a throaty purr that spurred him on. He kissed her urgently, feverishly, thoroughly, and still could not get enough. No woman had ever tasted so sweet, felt so warm, filled him with such searing need.

Roxie thrummed to the heated delirium of his kisses, his caresses, tingling and aching and swelling until she thought she would scream with wanting him. She felt dizzy, as if the world was spinning faster and faster around her. Desire charged up her chest, consuming her as she locked her arms around his neck and arched toward him, offering herself mind, heart, soul and body.

Her abrupt action caught Luke off guard and knocked him off balance. He started to fall back but managed to catch and right himself almost instantly. But the mishap served a purpose. It broke the keenly intense spell that had bound him as tight as chains. After a stunned second, he laughed.

Still easy in his embrace, Roxie leaned back a little and looked at him. The moonlight shone silvery on his features, dark and rugged and dangerous. She reached up and smoothed his haphazard black eyebrows. His hand came to her neck, and his thumb moved on her skin in small stirring circles. She closed her eyes and let herself drift on the sweet sensation.

The summer night air blew in and she shivered ever so slightly. He tightened his arms about her and drew her closer, into his heat and his scent. She wrapped her arms around his trim waist and snuggled against him contently, feeling warmed in heart as well as body.

They sat companionably, marveling at the moon and the stars and watching the lightning bugs that dotted the dark yard with twinkling pinpricks of light. Looking up, he pointed out the constellation called Orion with its three bright stars forming the Hunter's belt. In turn, she indicated her favorite, Queen Cassiopeia's five-starred throne. Other stars, some famous but most nameless, winked and blinked at them from afar. Dropping his lips into her hair, he told her how often he had yearned to see the stars without bars or screens blocking his view.

She shivered again, this time from the yearning to take all his hurts unto herself, to give him an unlimited view of the stars for all time, to help him erase the past and embrace the future. His mouth felt right and good within her hair. His arms lent her more than his warmth. They made her feel safe and secure in a way that was totally new to her.

When he lifted his head, she tilted hers to peer up at him, and what she found left her breathless. Never before had she seen him without his defensive mask in place. But now she saw vulnerability and fear and desire. And, yes, love.

"Luke," she said with a sigh.

His name was a soft endearment on her lips. Luke thrilled to the sound. He had no words in him to tell her how much. He smiled down at her. "Yes, Roxie?"

"Do you still find me fatiguing?"

"You know I don't."

"What then?" She blew the hint of a kiss over his mouth but skittered away before he could claim the substance of it. "What do you find me?"

"Stimulating," he said with no hesitation whatsoever. "Stimulating and seductive."

She laughed, low and throaty, and Luke could no longer keep from capturing her mouth. He kissed her and kissed her, angling his head this way and that, skimming his lips across her cheek to her ear and on down her throat to savor the smoothness of her skin, the salty taste of her, the sweet smell of her.

They broke apart only long enough to draw their breath and then fell upon each other again.

Roxie strained toward him, wishing to take in the length and the strength of him.

Luke tried to resist, tried to break away, but smoky desire held him fast.

His hands glided from her hip to her stomach to brush her breasts and then to hold them, caress them, finesse them. Her nipples stiffened against the delicate fabric of her dress, and he wondered how it would feel to fondle them with no clothing in between to restrict him. Her breath blew hot in his ear, calling his name over and over in a panting whisper that about drove him senseless.

"Luke . . . oh, Luke . . . please . . ."

He longed to tell her he loved her, tell her how good she felt, how much he ached for her. He wanted to reassure her that he would never hurt her, that he wished only to take care of her. But those were the sorts of things he could never say to her. All that he could not say he put into the fervent kisses he pressed upon her eyes, her cheeks, her lips, her throat.

Each kiss swept Roxie further into the vortex of her desires. She felt as if she'd been swept away by a tornado, swirling through a tempest of sensations. She no longer heard the leaves or the birds or the locusts symphonizing around her. She heard only the soft suction of their lips, the rasping catch of their breaths, the thundering gallop of their hearts. The slight chill in the air no longer nipped her skin. Her goose bumps rose solely from the tingling of her nerves to his touch. Her senses reeled and her body quivered, and she returned each of his kisses with a torrent of her own.

"I want you," she groaned on a husky note. "I want you and need you and want you."

Her impassioned words raged within Luke's blood until he thought his veins would burst from the intensity. He wanted her so desperately, the pleasure he felt was painful. He thought of her bed that he had seen only in his imagination but had pictured with snowy white sheets and plump feather pillows against which to lay her down and kiss her until she cried and took him into her. Then he thought of his own hard, narrow bed back at the boardinghouse, and it was as if the cool breeze of sanity swept over his back. He placed his hands on either side of her flushed cheeks and pulled her from him. Her eyes shimmered in the moonlight, and her face was a milky silhouette, her hair forming an aureole around it.

"Roxie," he whispered, regret lodging in his throat like a stone. "Roxie, we've got to—"

Fearing he would say what she did not want to hear, wanting this to go on and on and on into infinity, until those beautiful stars broke into a million pieces and fell from the sky, Roxie set the tips of her fingers on his lips and sighed unsteadily. "We've got each other, Luke," she said, "and we've got the rest of the night."

Luke kissed the pads of her fingers, lingering over each of them as if they were precious jewels. Then he lifted her hand and tenderly pressed his lips into the center of her palm. With agonizing deliberateness, he set her hand in her lap.

"We can't," he said, and there was a world of pain in his voice.

The heat surging through Roxie slowly banked. She sat up straight and fussed busily with her hair, her clothes. With a sinking heart she realized that her confession must have made a difference after all. His physical response had been obvious. She could only conclude he no longer wanted her because she no longer fit his image of her. She thought bitterly that she never should have told him her past secrets, that she should have let bygones be bygones. But she'd felt guilty, having him think her so perfect, so saintly. She should have let him go on believing the lie. Instead, she had knocked herself off her own pedestal.

"I guess I've disappointed you," she said stiffly.

Luke inhaled deeply. Desire still clamored, hammering at his head, pounding through his veins, throbbing within his loins.

He heard her, but her words scarcely made sense to his drumming ears.

"What?" he returned blankly.

"It's because of what I told you, isn't it?"

It took several seconds for her meaning to get through to him. When it finally did, he was stunned to realize that she could think something so completely and utterly wrong. He knew an incredulous expression came over his face as he repeated his first, stupefied response. "What?"

"It's because you think badly of me now that you know just how far from sainthood I really am." Roxie attempted a smile. Her mouth quivered. She sucked in her lower lip to stop its trembling. She wouldn't give him the satisfaction of her tears.

Luke stifled his second reaction, which was to suggest that she get her brains unscrambled, and said instead, "How in God's name could you ever think I'd think less of you—for any reason? I'm the last person in the world to judge others, but least of all, to judge you. Whatever happened, and I believe it was more his fault than yours, whatever happened doesn't dim you at all in my eyes. I know how good, how gentle, how fair—"

Roxie was still too despondent to comprehend what he was saying. She tried to blink away the tears that burned her eyes. Failing that, she let her lip slip from between her teeth and she began to cry. "I disappointed you. I'm not what you thought I was. I'm so much less—"

Again, Luke put his arms around her. Again, he comforted her with the warmth of his shoulder. Trying to soothe her, he rubbed her heaving back with his palm. And again, desire for her pulsated through him, demanding release. But this time his physical pangs were submerged in a great upswell of tenderness, in a surge of longing to ease her emotional suffering more than his physical torment.

"I could never think badly of you, Roxie," he told her in all honesty. "Never. No matter what you've done."

"It must have changed something." Pulling out of his arms, she sniffed back another large sob. "Otherwise, why don't you want me?"

"Don't want you?" If she had socked him in the gut, Luke couldn't have been more surprised. His breath whooshed out and his arms fell to his sides. Except for swallowing hard, he remained perfectly still, staring at her face.

She hung her head as if she was ashamed.

"My God, woman, don't you realize I'm throbbing with wanting you?" He took her shoulders between his hands, sorely tempted to try and shake some sense into her but simply held her in a light grip. "I'm sore from wanting you. I've wanted you so much, for so long, that all it takes is a whiff of your perfume—no, not even that. Just the thought of you. Just picturing your smile or remembering your laughter and I get so worked up, I ache with wanting."

Raising her head, Roxie gaped at him. The ardor in his voice was echoed on his face, in his eyes. "But what's wrong then? Why did you push me away?"

He released her and forked impatient fingers through his hair. "Because I can't let you get mixed up with me."

"But I want to be mixed up with you!" she cried in frustration.

"You don't understand what that means, Roxie," he said, and though he'd intended his tone to be mild, it came out dolefully harsh. "The looks, the talk—you had a taste of it at the carnival tonight."

"It was nothing!"

"Yes," he conceded, "it was nothing. But think about enduring it all the time, every day, wherever you go, because you're with me or associated with me. People talk—"

"I don't care what people say."

"No matter how much you tell yourself you don't care, you do," he corrected her grimly. "I know. I've suffered such talk my entire life."

"I'm not made of porcelain, Luke. I can handle it."

"You think that now because you don't fully realize what it can be like being isolated from everyone else, being socially unacceptable." He didn't know what more he could say to get her to understand. "You wouldn't be just Roxie Mitchell anymore. You'd be Roxie Mitchell, that Luke Bauer's woman. And that's if they were being kind."

Roxie personally thought being considered Luke Bauer's woman would suit her to a T, but she knew better than to tell him so—at least right now, anyway. "What I'd be is with you," she pointed out. "That's the important thing, not what anyone else might say about me."

To be with her—it sounded like all the dreams that had filled years of cold, lonely nights melded together into one glorious design. But that was the problem, Luke thought. It was only a dream. It could never be more than that.

"I want you, Roxie. I can't even begin to tell you how much I want you." He longed to stop there but steeled himself to go on. "But I care enough to want what's best for you. I can't let you make a foolish mistake. And Lord knows, getting mixed up with me would be a mistake that went way past foolish."

"Who are you to say what I can or can't do? If I want to make such a *mistake*"—she sneered the word—"how do you intend to stop me?"

"I'll find a way. I'll have to." He said it with determination. "I'll have to keep you from throwing yourself headlong into the mess I've made of my life. For your own good."

"Don't you start with that business." She bristled with indignation. "I'm sick and tired of everyone else knowing what's for my own good. Everyone thinks they can rule my life, *for my own good.* But I'm the only one who can say what's best for me. I'm the only one who knows what's in my heart." Roxie reached for him, longing to hold him and show him just what was in her heart.

Luke jerked out of her reach. He knew if he let her touch him it would be all over. He'd grab her, and the rest of the world be damned. But for her sake he fought the fire of his raging desires. And managed to insult her in the process. "Like you knew what was best for you in St. Louis?"

Her lungs emptied on a sharp gust. Her arms fell limply to her sides. "We're all capable of making mistakes," she said in a quiet voice. "You, of all people, should know that."

He came abruptly to his feet.

"Where are you going?" Roxie asked, not certain at the moment whether she really even cared.

"I need to walk a bit. I won't go far."

Feeling rejected and dejected, Roxie watched his silhouette fade into the darkness behind the schoolhouse. She sat listening to the wind rustle the leaves amid the myriad hum of night songs. The sky was filled with stars and striated with faint grayish wisps that with any luck would soon swell into rain clouds. She thought how ironic it was that when she finally made up her mind to love Luke Bauer, to brave all opposition, to face down all those who would have her suppress her feelings for her own good, Bauer, the lady-killer, should choose to be noble. *For her own good.*

It was one of those little ironies that sometimes made her feel that life was too complicated for her. At such times she couldn't even figure out what she felt, much less how to deal with it. She knew she was angry, terribly angry at all those who had ever made Luke feel so unwanted and unworthy. She knew she was disappointed, deeply disappointed, and a shade embarrassed, too, at having her advances rejected by him. She knew she was depressed, pervasively depressed, at his insistence on keeping her at arm's length. He could be more immutable than the Rock of Gibraltar when he set his mind to something. And it appeared he'd set his mind to setting her free.

"What do I do now?" she sighed into the shadows. She waited breathlessly, but the night returned no answer. When she heard his footfall, she jumped up to meet him face-to-face. But it wasn't his face she met. She met his mask, the detached, impenetrable mask that shielded his thoughts from the world.

"I want you to know that I do care for you, very much," he said on a note of finality that snuffed any hope she still harbored. "I've valued your friendship more than I can tell you. But I made a mistake in encouraging you as I have. Besides alienating you from your family and friends—"

"That's not entirely true," she interrupted. "Granted, my brothers have behaved like asses. But my parents haven't said word one against you. And my friends like me despite my . . ." She groped for the right phrase.

"Your lack of judgment?"

She was glad it was too dark for him to see her flush. "Despite whether or not they agree with me a hundred percent, about anything."

Luke didn't think he could stand much more of this. His soul was shattering, and he feared that all too soon his control would shatter with it. He had to convince her to drop it, and now.

"Our friendship has been . . . frustrating . . . for me," he said in a purposely toneless voice. "For my good as much as for yours, I think we'd do best to call a halt to it."

This was worse, far worse, than anything Roxie had feared. She'd never expected him to tell her it was over between them. As her mouth fell open, her fingers flew up to hold back any cries that might try to escape.

"You—you can't mean that," she finally stammered.

"It's for the best."

His voice was without inflection, his expression completely blank. It was clear to her that he was deaf to any pleading or reasoning she might try to make. Turning on her heel, she started back to her car. She climbed in on the driver's side and, a minute or so later, he joined her in the passenger seat. They drove off wordlessly.

And a night that had begun with such wonderful promise ended with wrenching pain.

Muffling the closing of the back door as much as she could, Roxie removed her white shoes and crossed the kitchen on cat's feet. Adroitly maneuvering in a zigzag pattern to avoid the creakiest steps, she mounted the staircase, then paused, listening tensely at the top. The house was blanketed in sleep. She snuck into the sanctuary of her room in relief.

She felt like an errant teenager, tiptoeing in after staying out too late with her boyfriend. She winced at the image. Luke had said the old schoolhouse was where he'd taken all the girls to pitch a little woo. He still did, she qualified gloomily. She wondered if he kept a scorecard, and just to rub a little more salt into her wound, figured she had probably rated a zero.

She hurt. Heaven above, how she hurt! She had thought that Arthur had left her immune to such gnawing pain. But this was much worse than anything she'd felt then. With Arthur, her misery had been mitigated somewhat by an underscoring relief. Deep down she'd been glad to get out of it. She felt no such relief now. All she felt was pure unadulterated heartache.

Her dress slid to the floor in a crinkling hush. Uncharacteristically, she let it lay, stepping over its folds to drop her underclothes alongside it. So despondent she could hardly lift her arms over her head, she donned her crinkly cotton nightgown. Then she slid beneath snowy white sheets and huddled in a tight ball, determined never to think of Luke Bauer again.

Naturally she thought of him. She pressed her cheek into her palm and thought of her last sight of him, on that dry, rutted road that led to the local bootlegger. He had insisted she drop him there rather than drive him back to the boardinghouse.

Against all her resolutions not to, she had pleaded, "Please, Luke, don't go down that road."

For her pains she had received a defiant stare that curdled her blood, and she stared out at the trees standing in dense relief against the night sky, determined not to make a fool of herself over another man. But this wasn't just another man. This was Luke Bauer, the man she loved.

As light as a dandelion puff dancing on the wind, his fingertip had brushed her cheek. His defiance had receded, replaced by a sorrowful expression that had reflected her own.

"Don't worry about me, Roxie" he had said through barely moving lips. "It's not worth your time. I can take care of myself."

"Like you have in the past?" she'd shot back.

The corner of his mouth had crooked in a bittersweet smile meant to mask his pain. "Tit for tat, hey? Well, let me assure you I intend to take much better care of myself in the future. As soon as I've got enough money together I'm going to leave here and start over somewhere else."

She hadn't responded, only looked at him with a stricken expression.

"Just as soon as I can afford it, I'm gone," he had reiterated as he reached for the car's door.

She'd watched him get out. He'd looked back, and their eyes had locked.

"You'll take care of yourself, won't you?" he had asked.

"Yes," she had said on a filament of breath.

"Be sure you do."

With that, he had closed the car door, turned his back on her

and started down the road to perdition. She'd driven off with
her gaze straight ahead but hadn't been able to keep from looking back just once. Though her vision blurred, she'd clearly
seen him square his shoulders and stick his hands in his pockets
as he disappeared into the darkness.

Now she coiled on her bed and wondered and worried. Had
he bought a bottle from the bootlegger? Would he get drunk
and do something stupid? Something that would cause him to
be sent back to prison? She worried until she shook with
released sobs, then furiously asked herself why she cared
anyway. She didn't give a hoot about Luke Bauer and never
had.

When she couldn't convince herself of that, when the memory
of his every word, his every touch, his every kiss would not leave
her be, she let the tears fall, soaking her plump pillow and
saturating her grieving soul.

The first thing Luke became aware of was the spinning. The
bed was spinning viciously. He opened his eyes. Not the bed.
The room. It was going round and round like a tumbleweed
caught in a twister. He closed his eyes and groaned. It didn't
help. He lay very still and prayed for a quick and merciful death.

Later, he woke a second time and discovered that though the
bed and the room had stopped spinning, his stomach had taken
up the slack. It heaved violently. He scrambled up off the bed
and down the hall to the bathroom he shared with four other
boarders. Fortunately it was unoccupied, and he didn't have to
wait to empty his stomach of its severe distress.

Still later, as he sat on the side of the bed and dressed with
shaking hands, he struggled to remember where he had gotten
drunk and with whom. Not with Roxie, that much he knew.
Because his last clear memory was of her profile, frozen into

remote dispassion as she pulled away from the corner of the road.

*What corner of what road?* he wondered now, and began groping around under the bed for his shoes. His hand hit something made of glass and sent it rolling into the middle of the room. It was a jar with a metal screw-top lid. A murky liquid sloshed wildly in the bottom. It reminded him too vividly of his stomach, and he shut his eyes again.

And then he remembered.

He remembered the wonderful evening, the beauty of the night enhanced by the beauty of Roxie. He remembered the feel of her, the creamy texture of her skin, the silken softness of her hair. He remembered the rosewater scent that grew stronger with her ardor and the passionate fervor that heightened with each kiss. He remembered, and he felt himself warming with the memories.

He opened his eyes and slowly bent to pick up the almost-empty jar. He remembered, then, which corner of which road. Remembered, too, the way the rotgut whiskey he'd swilled had made his eyes water, his nose run, and his throat burn. It was the worst-tasting, most potent stuff he'd ever put a lip on, and he'd erroneously figured it was the best way to help him forget what had transpired.

The end of the evening had been the end of his dreams and the beginning of his descent into a drunken hell. He had done what he had to do, for Roxie's sake, but it had cost him dearly. It would be so much more lonely going on without her now than it would have been had he never met her.

As if to add to his suffering, the church bells rang. In his mind's eye he could see her dressed in her Sunday best. He imagined how the morning sun would glimmer in the honey-gold strands of her hair as she climbed the steps to attend the weekly worship service. He pictured her sweet face turned to the front as she sat in the pew between her mother and father, listening to the preacher's sermon. He heard her clear voice singing one of those old-time hymns he remembered from his childhood.

What would she pray for? When she bowed her head, would she pray for him and for his salvation? Or would she simply ask the Lord to help her forget she'd ever met a heathen such as himself?

A spurt of rage shook him. How he wished he'd never met her! How he wished he'd never come back to Blue Ridge! But in addition to everything else, he'd had some wild and crazy idea about moving into his grandfather's old house, rolling up his sleeves and working the orchard and tending the beehives. Foolishly he'd thought he might even gain a measure of respect from the townspeople in the process.

It had been a mistake, coming back, another damned act of pride that had ultimately backfired on him. Hadn't he learned by now he didn't have to prove anything to anyone else? He only had to prove himself to himself.

So what had he proven? He'd proven he could still drink like a fish. Or like his father. The difference being he could quit and his father never could. To prove that last, he straightened and, on legs that felt like the marrow had been sucked out of the bones, weaved back to the bathroom, where he poured the contents of the jar down the drain and then tossed the empty into the wastebasket under the sink. For all the good it had done him, he had at least had the sense to bring the stuff back to his room and drink alone. More important, he'd stayed away from trouble, even if he hadn't achieved anything more worthwhile than a head-pounding, stomach-churning, knee-wobbling hangover.

He'd also proven that he couldn't drown his misery in alcohol. That was the worst part of it. Because this was the unsinkable kind of misery, the kind you had to learn to live with, day in and day out.

Back in his room, he stretched out on his bed, which to his great relief remained motionless, and offered up a prayer of thanks that he had the day to sober up before he had to go to work. Not that he could keep his drunken night a secret. There were no secrets in Blue Ridge. That was how he'd known where to find the bootlegger. He'd overheard some of the fellows in the warehouse talking about where he was located and what he sold, and he guessed he must have tucked the information away in the back of his mind.

By now half the town probably knew he'd visited the bootlegger last night, and they were probably busy enlightening the other half. That was how it went around here. What one knew, everyone else soon would. How he yearned to get away from it all, from the prying eyes and the pointing fingers, from the ongoing censure and the unending gossip.

He remembered telling Roxie he intended to leave town and start fresh somewhere else. It would be the best thing for both of them. Eventually, people would forget he even existed and forgive her for daring to give him a chance. Yes, the farther he got from her, the better. Maybe the misery that the liquor couldn't blot would fade with distance.

But he needed money to start somewhere new, and though he lived frugally, he hadn't saved nearly enough. He was stuck in Blue Ridge for the time being. Stuck with the continual reminders of Roxie and the aching and the wanting and the loneliness.

If he just had the money, he'd get away from it all.

# CHAPTER 12

It was hard to say which was worse, the heat or the humidity, Roxie mused. Regardless, a storm was brewing. And it promised to be a big one if those low clouds filling every inch of the sky and the close, almost suffocating air were anything to go by.

Just as bad was the effect it was having on everyone's mood at work. Lana unreasonably snapped at Vicky within five minutes of her arrival and the two fumed in antagonistic silence the rest of the morning. Barbara accidentally spilled her cup of coffee over a stack of letters she had just finished typing and snarled if anyone so much as glanced at her. Fesol had shut himself in his office to try to reconcile, at Roxie's request, the inventory and audit numbers from last week's ledger that, no matter how often she had reworked them, were not computing as they should have and which had totally messed up her book-keeping for the month. Even the normally genial Gary was grumpy as an old bear, growling at anyone and everyone who set foot in the warehouse.

It occurred to Roxie as she watched all these dynamics play out that a good storm might clear the air inside as well as outside the warehouse. She didn't say it aloud, however, as her apathy outweighed her annoyance. That was the reason she had asked Fesol to check the ledger, something she normally wouldn't dream of doing. But she couldn't get worked up enough to care, not about her job, not about her life, and certainly not about those numbers. More than a week had

passed since her evening with Luke, and she still couldn't find
an interest in anything.

"I'm sorry, Mr. Stewart," she said listlessly when he complained to her about the way everyone had been acting this
morning.

His eyes widened with distress behind his spectacles. "Oh,
no, not you too. I can't stand it."

"Stand what?" Roxie asked, her tone heavy with indifference.

"This widespread attack of Monday-morning blahs."

Roxie shrugged.

His wooden swivel chair creaked as he leaned back in it, slid
his thumbs under those red suspenders of his, and cast a disappointed look at her. "I was counting on you to be the ray of
sunshine amidst all the doom and gloom around here."

"I'm sorry, Mr. Stewart," she said again.

He sat up abruptly, dismissing her with an abrupt wave and a
terse order. "Don't come back in here until Tuesday. And don't
let anyone else in here today, either. I can't stand Mondays like
this."

It amazed Roxie to find that her feet were moving one after
the other, carrying her back to her office, when her body felt
like deadweight. She concentrated on this astounding accomplishment, watching each step her feet made. It took effort,
but by dint of focusing her thoughts on her amazing feet, she
was able, for a moment, to elude the continual hounds of her
"what ifs."

What if she refused to give in? What if she went to Luke and
told him straight out that she loved him? What if she told him
she wasn't going to give up without a fight? What if she said she
would follow him to the ends of the earth? What if she dogged
his heels the way thoughts of him dogged her?

Feet, she reminded herself. She should be thinking about her
poor feet, having to haul around this sluggish uncooperative

body. She looked down past her dull gray skirt to her sensible black pumps, sensibly taking her to her office, and came to a crashing halt as she smashed head-on into a masculine chest.

Socks and shirts of every size and color showered over her. Two boxes went flying and then hit the floor with thumping plops. A highly descriptive expletive reverberated in the air.

"Sorry," Willie Newcomer grumbled as he righted himself. He didn't sound very sorry. He sounded thoroughly disgusted. He looked even more so as he inspected the array of clothing littering the floor.

"I'm the sorry one," Roxie said. "I wasn't watching where I was going."

He gave her a glance that clearly said, why the hell not? But he didn't say a word. Bending he began scooping socks and shirts into the boxes in willy-nilly fashion. They would have to be sorted and refolded later, before they were shipped, but for now this would have to do.

Roxie plucked a pair of men's black dress socks off the shoulder of her pale gray pleated blouse and gave them to him. Then she stooped to help him retrieve the rest. As she picked up the last shirt, she again apologized.

"Forget it," he growled, sounding as if he would remember it until his dying day.

"Okay." The message she wanted him to deliver to his girlfriend popped into her head then. "But would you do me a favor and tell Margaret—"

"Don't mention Margaret Clark to me," he interrupted brusquely. "Not today. Not ever again."

That said, he snatched the shirt she was still holding from her hand and stomped on down the corridor. Roxie gaped at his back until he disappeared around the corner. Great, she thought. On top of everything else, a lovers' quarrel.

It must be the wrong time of year for lovers, she decided with a mental sigh. Romance seemed to be in a mid-summer slump. Maybe if she waited until next spring, Luke would be more compliant. She thought of spring, of the joyful rejuvenation of nature, the planting of crops and the birthing of farm animals, the blossoming flowers and budding trees. She spun a ridiculous daydream of sprinkling wild flower petals over Luke's dark, glossy hair, of raining a kiss for every petal . . .

Another sigh, this one glumly audible, accompanied her into the refuge of her own office. She ought to know better than to permit such dreams to enter her head. Dreams led to disappointments, and she'd had enough disappointments to last her the rest of her life.

She sank into her chair to wait, then realized she had no idea what she was waiting for. Giving herself a good shake, she reached for the small stack of paid receipts that had been left on her desk and began entering them in this week's ledger.

If asked, not a single employee at Stewart's Warehouse would have thought Monday afternoon could possibly be worse than that Monday morning. If so asked, every employee would have been wrong. Directly after lunch a minor accident on the dock sent two of Gary's loaders home for the day, shifting an extra burden onto everyone else. Then one of the pickers up and quit without notice, leaving Gary even more short-handed than before.

He ranted for a good five minutes to Roxie, who finally worked up enough concern to demand to know why Fesol had not yet returned the ledger she had asked him to check.

"Because," he explained icily, "I haven't balanced it yet."

"So get it balanced," she snapped, and both stamped back to their respective offices, their doors slamming one right after the other.

An hour later Fesol charged into her office with the ledger

and another sheet of paper under his arm and insisted she accompany him to Layton Stewart's office. She warned him that it wasn't such a good idea and asked if this could wait until tomorrow, but Fesol was adamant that it had to be taken care of today. Grudgingly, she followed him down the hall.

Judging by the frown that furrowed his brow, Layton Stewart wasn't too happy to see either one of them.

Ignoring that frown as well as the fact that it really should have been Roxie who was pursuing this discrepancy, Fesol laid the ledger in the center of their boss's desk, stabbed a long, skinny finger at a column of figures and said triumphantly, "There. Right there."

Layton Stewart painstakingly lifted his employee's finger and removed it from his sight before perusing the itemized figures. Roxie clasped her hands together and studied them, trying to recount precisely how many days, weeks, months, it had taken her to stop pining for Arthur. She estimated, then doubled, tripled the figure—her estimate for how long her heart would grieve for Luke.

"What's where?" Layton Stewart finally asked Fesol.

The payroll clerk huffed out a sigh to underscore his annoyance with the entire situation. "There." He leaned forward and indicated a credit figure. "That's the imbalance that Roxie couldn't find."

Layton Stewart looked up at him. "So?"

"So it doesn't correspond with the deposit receipts." Fesol spread out the separate accounting sheet he had prepared on top of the ledger. He indicated a difference of slightly over one hundred dollars in the total amount.

Frowning now, Roxie sidled around the desk to study the figures. She was doing her best to understand what they were saying. But she'd been in this fog for over a week and felt like she would never understand anything again, no matter how hard she tried.

"First I checked the ledger item by item against the ladings," Fesol continued. "Then, just to make sure I hadn't missed anything, I went through the ledger from front to back and found this." With a flourish he produced a thin blue piece of paper. A square of smeary red ink read PAID IN FULL. Beneath that, handwritten in, was the word CASH. The amount corresponded to the penny with the figure on the accounting sheet. It was slightly over one hundred dollars more than the sum of the bank deposits.

"Where was that?" Roxie couldn't recall ever seeing it before.

"Stuck in the back, behind the last page."

Thinking the problem had been resolved, Roxie inched toward the door. "I'll just be going—"

"Hold on a minute." Layton Stewart gestured imperiously. "You need to see what this is about."

Roxie had no choice but to obey his order and return to the desk. She didn't care to know what it was about. She didn't care about anything. Didn't anyone around here understand that?

Taking the blue lading sheet in hand, the warehouse owner examined it closely. It was dated exactly a week earlier, the previous Monday. By all rights, it should have been caught by Roxie when she was preparing last week's ledger for his perusal. But that was her first day back at work after her fiasco with Luke and she had obviously fallen down on the job.

"Another Monday mess," he muttered under his breath and then glanced up at Fesol. "I assume that you've told no one else about this discrepancy."

The statement was in actuality a question, and Fesol promptly assured his employer that he'd told no one. He gazed down his long nose at Roxie in a way that made her feel totally incompetent and then looked back at Layton Stewart. "I naturally wished to call it to the attention of the two of you before drawing any conclusions."

But it was perfectly obvious that he had already drawn a conclusion. And it was the only conclusion that seemed logical. No one uttered the word, but Roxie knew they were all thinking it.

"Naturally," Layton Stewart said in a tone intended to sooth the clerk's offended sensibilities. "Please continue to keep this matter to yourself for the time being. I intend to make a thorough inquiry."

"Of course." With a brisk nod, Fesol made his exit.

Harmonizing with the click of the door, Layton Stewart heaved a melancholy sigh. "He'll expect a raise for this, I'm sure."

"I don't know how I missed that," Roxie murmured, more to herself than to him. But in fact she did know. She had been too engrossed in her personal problems to properly do the job she was being paid to do.

Patting the chair beside his desk, Layton Stewart told her to sit down. "You've been moping around here for over a week now."

She slumped there in a dejected heap. "I know."

"Whatever it is that's bothering you will just have to be shelved for the time being," he said. "I'd like to help you, even tell you to take some time off to get back on track, but this has to come first. We can't let a possible embezzlement wait for anything."

Though he'd spoken kindly, his speech was lashed with enough of a sting to prick her out of her mood. "Thank you, Mr. Stewart, but I'll cope. As you say, this matter must come first." A disquieting chill snaked up her spine. "Do you really think it could be . . . embezzlement?"

"I don't know." He looked down at the ledger. "As you well

know, the entries in here are taken from the ladings, so the first thing, I suppose, is to find out who accepted payment on this shipment last week and how much was actually received."

"And who tucked it in the back of the ledger," she added.

"Then we'll need to determine who made the bank deposit that day." He picked up the blue lading. "I'll give you the easy one. You check this out."

Roxie took it and stood. "I'll get right on it."

"Be as discreet as you can—even though I know this will be all over the warehouse in a matter of minutes," he said gloomily.

As she went out she could hear him grumble, "Mondays."

All paperwork was supposed to be signed by whichever employee handled it. Although she had been working at the warehouse long enough to recognize some of the signatures, she couldn't always read every one of them. Whether it was because they were in a hurry or because they had really poor penmanship, people sometimes scrawled something resembling hen scratches across the bottom. That was the problem with this one. It was impossible to tell who had signed it.

Roxie walked to Gary's office. As she wended her way through the warehouse, she looked up and down the aisles but did not find Luke. She wasn't certain whether she was disappointed or relieved.

She found Gary at his desk, barking into the telephone. "Hell, I'm sorry, but with two of my men out and one having just quit, I'm backlogged here. All I can tell you is that your order will get out as soon as I can get it out."

While he continued his conversation she tried not to survey anything beyond the glass window that looked out into the warehouse. She failed miserably. Her gaze continually flicked, searching, seeking, and, at last, finding. Luke strode down a row, coming closer and closer. Her heart lurched painfully. Then he turned abruptly and disappeared from view. It had just been a glimpse, but it hurt. After nine days it surprised her that the wound could feel so agonizingly fresh.

"What can I do for you?" Gary asked, sounding as harried as he looked.

Jolted out of her misery, she handed him the lading bill. "Can you tell me who received the payment on that? I can't read the signature."

He glanced at it, then at her, his eyes narrowing. "Is there a problem I should know about?"

"We don't know yet," she replied, wondering why she suddenly felt like she was in the wrong. "I'd like to speak with whoever handled this."

"Today?"

"Yes."

"We're pretty rushed today, what with the—"

"Today," she broke in firmly. "It's important."

After a long pause he stepped to the door and hollered out into the warehouse, "Bauer! I need to see you for a minute."

The hair on the back of Roxie's neck stood on end. Thunder boomed like a beaten drum and the dock workers dashed inside as the skies opened up and the rain poured down. She stared at Gary and moved her mouth soundlessly. Luke!

The storm had broken.

He stopped at the door of Gary's cubicle. His eyes flashed silver when he saw her, but quickly dulled to a lusterless lead. Gary excused himself and Roxie had to fight to keep from flinging herself on him, wildly begging him to stay. She looked down, around, anywhere but at Luke. But it didn't matter whether she looked at him or not. Her nerves hummed with awareness of him.

Finally he said, "You wanted to see me about something?"

Caution muted his tone. She darted a look and saw that he

held himself warily, alert for trouble. Hating having to do this, she gave him the bill. "Did you accept this payment?"

He didn't even glance at it. "You must know I did, or you would be asking somebody else."

She bit her lower lip. "Please, Luke, don't make this any more difficult for me than it already is."

After checking the lading, he handed it back to her. "Yes, I received it. Last Monday."

She riveted her gaze to the figure written on the bill. Swallowing hard, she wished she didn't have to ask him anything else. "Did—did you actually receive the full amount?"

The silence battered at her until she had to give up and look at him. He met her gaze with an empty stare. She balanced on the precipice of anguished doubt a few seconds longer, then crumpled the bill in her fist and fled.

At the back of her mind she was dimly aware that the dock workers who had come in from the rain had observed the entire exchange through the glass window, but she couldn't worry about that now. She was too busy trying to cope with all the ugly suspicion and piercing doubt that mauled her. Her heart, her soul, her very being, rejected even the remotest suggestion that Luke could have taken that money. But like the snake in the Garden of Eden, her mind twisted her faith. He'd told her, hadn't he, that all he needed was money to get out of town. It would have been so easy to pocket the cash.

*No!* She fiercely repelled such a shameful supposition. He couldn't, he wouldn't. She returned to her office, determined to believe it.

Within the hour, the rumor blazed through the company. Money—some said as much as a thousand dollars—was missing, and Luke Bauer had been questioned about it.

Roxie couldn't bear the rash of accusatory whispers that erupted all around her. She hid in the ladies' room but didn't lock the door. She was still there when Barbara burst in, tearfully denying any wrongdoing. She turned to Roxie and said, "All I did was take the packet and deposit slip to the bank after Mr. Stewart added it up!"

The door swung open again, and Barbara angrily swiped her hands over her tear-blotched cheeks before facing Lana and Vicky Sue. "And you two just better not say anything to me ever again. The way you looked at me as if . . . as if I were a thief or something!"

"We didn't mean anything like that," Lana soothed. "We know you're nothing of the kind."

"Besides," Vicky Sue put in, "we all know who's really guilty."

Roxie's hackles rose instantly. She rounded on the woman standing by the sink and demanded coldly, "Just what do you mean by that?"

"Well, surely, you can't believe—"

"I'll tell you what I believe. I believe you're spreading a viscous rumor without just cause. We haven't even determined that anything other than an honest mistake has taken place. Without a crime, I don't see how anyone can be considered guilty."

Vicky Sue's face reddened with indignation at being singled out. "Fesol told us that it was as open and shut a case as he'd ever seen."

"And Willie says you've already questioned Luke Bauer about it," Barbara said with a sniff. "So why try to defend him?"

"We all knew when you hired him you were making a mistake," Lana stated on a righteous note that made Roxie's palm itch to slap her.

Instead, giving them all one furiously contemptuous look, she stalked out. She went directly to Layton Stewart's office, entering without bothering to knock. "Mr. Stewart, something's got to be done."

"I think I'm going to cut Mondays out of my calendar," he grumbled without looking up from the ledger he was still studying. "What is it now?"

"Fesol has accused Luke of taking the money and even said it was an open and shut case."

Real consternation sobered Layton Stewart's grandfatherly features. Saying he'd better have a talk with the payroll clerk, he rose from his chair, and together he and Roxie went to find him. On the way, Roxie explained all that she'd learned in the ladies' room.

"Everyone just assumes he's guilty, without even giving him a chance," she concluded.

"It's true we can't make such baseless assumptions about him," the warehouse owner agreed. "But neither can we blindly assume he is not guilty."

The words rang like a death knell. They tolled so loudly in Roxie's heart she did not even derive the least satisfaction from hearing Layton Stewart inform Fesol in no uncertain terms that if he expressed one more opinion, just one, about what may or may not have been done by whom, it would mean his job.

"Not so much as a syllable," he ordered with rare anger.

For once Fesol gave the appearance of sincerely apologizing. But Roxie hardly noticed. The what-ifs had returned to haunt her. What if Luke had really done it? What if he'd taken the money to get away from her? What if he had planned it all along? What if? Her fear escalated with each what-if that persecuted her.

She trailed Layton Stewart into Gary's office with a desolate heart. This was the worst nightmare she'd ever lived, far worse than the awful day she had learned Arthur's wife was pregnant and realized that he had just been using her. This was worse than any nightmare. Nightmares end. This was going on and on until she thought she would scream.

Gary and Luke awaited them. Even as they entered, Gary spoke up. "I want to go on record as saying I've got complete faith in Luke Bauer. I've let every worker in my warehouse know how I feel, and I'm ready to say the same to anyone else."

"That's high praise, coming from you," Layton Stewart said.

Though she remained silent, Roxie wanted to throw the foreman a wealth of roses. At least one person supported her belief that Luke must be innocent.

Layton Stewart offered Luke his hand. After a perceptible delay, he took it. "I want to apologize to you," the warehouse owner said in his direct way. "I sincerely regret the unfounded accusations to which you've been subjected. But the sooner we can get to the bottom of this, the sooner we'll have the rumors cleared out and dumped in the trash bin where they belong."

In her heart Roxie begged Luke not use a sarcastic tone, not to be coldly defiant.

He nodded and said. "I'll do whatever is necessary to help you find out what happened, Mr. Stewart."

"I appreciate your cooperation. And your understanding."

"It's only natural that you'd talk to me, sir. I was the last to handle that particular shipment."

With a brisk nod, Layton Stewart got down to business and began grilling him on the receipt of the lading.

Roxie stared in wide-eyed admiration. Despite his tensed stance, despite his closed expression, Luke replied to every question with reasoned calm. How difficult it must be for him, she could only guess, but she knew his self-possession couldn't come easily. Her heart swelled with pride . . . and love.

Unexpectedly, he looked her way. For a heartbreaking instant, the guard slipped. His gray eyes clouded with pain and longing and uncertainty. Her own eyes blurred with tears as she lifted a hand toward him. The shutter closed. He withdrew into his impenetrable shell. When Layton Stewart dismissed him, he didn't even glance Roxie's way. He simply pivoted and strode out.

Five o'clock crawled in at long last. Roxie felt as if she'd been through every emotion known to humankind, with a few extras thrown in for experimentation. Layton Stewart's assurances that they would get the matter settled as quickly as possible hadn't encouraged her in the least.

Part of her feared the solution. As much as she wanted to believe otherwise, a nasty, nagging suspicion that maybe Luke had taken the money would not be stilled. She felt she would never be sure until she heard it from his own lips, until he told her, "I didn't do it."

She was almost home when, on impulse, she made a U-turn and headed back the other direction, past the train tracks and into the section of town where the houses looked as old as time. She had no clear notionwhat she meant to do. She only knew that she could not let another night pass without some understanding between them. Nine days of wordless pretense had been bad enough. This new barrier was unendurable.

She parked in front of the boardinghouse where Luke lived and then sat there for a moment, gathering her courage. An overcoat of guilt hung on her as she recalled the day's events and the part she had played in them. Finally realizing she couldn't put this off any longer, she got out of the car and, with no umbrella to protect her, ran through the falling rain and across the freshly painted porch into the house.

A kerosene lamp burned on the entry table. The smell of cauliflower from the evening meal being prepared in the kitchen at the back of the house assaulted her nostrils. A worn flowered runner muffled her footsteps as she climbed the stairs to the second floor.

In a narrow hall, facing the door with her knuckles raised,

Roxie suffered an attack of nerves so severe she almost turned tail and ran. She pulled her hand back and plucked at the damp crepe of her blouse that clung to her skin. What could she say? Luke wouldn't welcome her interference, and she knew she couldn't stand any more of that indifferent attitude he put on. But one thing kept her from leaving.

Love. If anything, she loved him more than ever. Every protective instinct she possessed rushed to the fore. She wasn't going to let him go through this alone. Whatever he may have done, she was going to help him through it. Whether he wanted her or not, he needed her. And she loved him too much to turn away.

She knocked. Closing her eyes, she took in as many deep breaths as she could.

The door wrenched open.

"What are you doing here?" he demanded.

She opened her eyes. He stood there, filling the doorway with his broad shoulders. He was still wearing his work clothes, a blue shirt and jeans. His hair was charmingly mussed, his face uncharmingly remote.

"That's not a very friendly welcome," she said.

"I'm not feeling very friendly."

"Please, Luke, I just want to talk."

He held the door as if ready to slam it in her face. She wondered if she would have to resort to climbing through his window in order to talk to him. With an abrupt movement he suddenly stepped back and flung open the door.

"Suit yourself," he said in that apathetic tone she hated.

His room was small and spare, with a ratty throw rug covering part of the bare floor, a cracked ceiling with a bare light bulb glaring down, and a stained shade pulled halfway up in the curtainless window. A chest of drawers in need of refinishing, a ladder-backed chair and an iron-framed bed were the only furnishings. To Roxie, it looked depressingly Spartan.

"It's larger and cleaner than any cell," he said.

She spun around to face him. His eyes were like ashes, cold and gray. Her heart lodged hard in her throat.

They were so different, so completely different. He was so dark and defensive; she so fair and vulnerably open. He distrusted love, happiness, all the things he'd never known. She had faith in the certainty of life's blessings while he sometimes seemed to curse the day he was born. Would they be able to bridge those differences? It would take effort, a lot of effort on both their parts. Did she have what it took to try? Did he?

Luke jerked away, breaking the invisible lock that had held them together. He crossed to the window, set his hands on the frame, and studied the wet street. Her heart pounding, she waited. He wheeled around.

"Well, aren't you going to ask me if I did it?" he challenged, his strong hands clenching and unclenching at his sides. "Isn't that why you came?"

All the courage she'd gathered and the conviction she held surged into her voice. "No. I don't have to ask. I know you didn't."

He stared at her for so long she thought she might faint from the almost sickening apprehension building inside her. Then he extended his hand. Without hesitation, she rushed to take it.

# CHAPTER 13

Luke took her hand, his fingers curling over hers to tug her closer. Gazing into her blue eyes, he saw them shining with what he'd so often yearned to see—love. Soft, glowing, acquiescent love. He bent his lips to her hand and pressed a kiss into her palm. Then he raised his head.

"Loving me won't be easy," he warned her.

His gray eyes flashed as the lightning outside danced in their depths. "Love is never easy," she said softly. "Not the lasting kind of love."

Luke moved his lips to the pulse point of her wrist, feeling it beat frenetically for him.

Roxie played lightly with his dark hair, letting strands of it drift through her fingers.

Their eyes met, and for an exquisite eternity neither dared move.

Then the pain of denial would no longer be borne. After turning off the harsh overhead light, Luke lifted her into his arms and carried her to his bed. Its rusty springs squeaked as he settled their weight on it. Roxie scarcely noted the lumpy mattress, the squealing springs, the stark surroundings. She was aware only of him, of his body squeezed in next to hers.

"You're wet," he said, just now noticing.

She lifted her hand and laid it against his cheek. "I forgot my umbrella."

He squinted, half smiling. "Has anyone ever told you that

you're beautiful when you're wet?"

She pursed her lips. "I do believe you're the first."

He reached over and pulled down the window shade, his eyes glittering possessively in the semi-darkness. "And the last."

"And the last," she echoed in a voice that left no room for doubt.

Luke touched her slowly, reverently, not quite able to believe she was real. He'd had so many fantasies, so many frustrations. He feared he would blink and she would be gone. But this was no fantasy. She was real and warm and overwhelmingly exciting.

In his fantasies he'd been a terrific lover, wildly satisfying all the nameless, faceless women of the lost years. More recently, his dreams had been of Roxie, but her reaction had been the same. For her he'd been the perfect lover. But this was not a dream. She lay beside him, her breath mingling with his, and he knew he might not be the perfect lover. As out of practice as he was, he might not be much of a lover at all.

While his mouth explored the delicate bone of her jaw and the heated pulsing of her throat, he tried to quell the fear rising alongside his need. She wound her arms around his neck and sighed encouragingly in his ear. He hesitated, then swept his palm downward to the sensitive peak of her breast. His fingers searched through the pleats of the crepe of her blouse, down to her stomach and back, but he could find no buttons. His fear that he might not satisfy her grew by leaps and bounds. He couldn't even find the damn buttons!

Lost in the rippling pleasure of that palm gliding over her breasts, those fingertips wandering through her pleats, Roxie didn't at first realize what he was doing. But pressed as she was against him, she could feel the change in the tension of his muscles, and she finally comprehended his problem. She caught his hand and slid it beneath her, shifting slightly as she guided him to where her blouse buttons were.

"They're in the back," she told him.

"It's been a long time," he rasped.

"Forever," she agreed. "I've waited for you forever."

Her slender back warmed Luke's palm. The pearl buttons cooled his fingertips. He gazed down at her face, softened with love for him, and a new fear took hold of him. "Too long," he grated. "It's been too long for me. I'm afraid I'll go too fast. Afraid I'll hurt—"

Roxie shushed him with a tender kiss. Her being flooded with a love such as she'd never before known, a love more radiant in the giving than in the receiving. She stroked the strong line of his jaw with her fingertip, letting him feel as well as see how much she loved him.

"We'll go slowly," she whispered against his lips, "slowly into the night."

Her understanding nearly undid him. In a voice raw with emotion, he said, "I need you, Roxie."

Her heart went out to him. "I need you, too, Luke. I need you, and I love you."

"All my life I've needed you." He brushed her damp hair off her face, sifted through it with his fingers. "Years and years of needing and wishing and—"

"I'm here now." She wrapped him within the comfort of her arms, wanting to fill the void inside him, erase from his past all the time he had needed loving and went lacking. "Now and always."

He looked at her with an intensity that made her dizzy. "All those wishes—I never dreamed they could be fulfilled so completely. I never dared dream of a woman like you. You're my every dream, Roxie."

"And you, mine," she said with hushed happiness.

Thunder rattled through the room as they kissed deeply,

deliciously, deliriously. One of his hands slid to the small of her back and pulled her against him so she could feel how hard he was for her while the other caressed her breast through her blouse. She matched him touch for touch, gliding the pads of her fingers over his eyebrows, his cheeks, his chin, as if to convince herself that he was truly there, that they were really together at long last.

When they broke apart to catch their breath, Roxie unbuttoned his shirt and pushed it off his shoulders, running her hands along his arms, muscular from months of warehouse work. She feathered light kisses down his chest to his stomach and back up again, reveling in the smell and taste of his skin, relishing the feel of his hard flesh.

In turn, Luke trailed his fingers along the length of her spine, opening her buttons until her crepe blouse fell away from her body, bunching the hem of the plain satin slip in his hands and working it up and over her head so he could see her in the flesh.

The rest of their clothing came off in bits and pieces, between caresses that sent them soaring and kisses that spiraled deeper, deeper, carrying them further into the world of pure sensation.

She smiled up at him. "Your hands are hot on my skin."

He rubbed his knuckles down her cheek. "It's you who makes them hot."

Roxie combed her fingers through his hair when he bent his head to her breasts. A shock of pleasure arched her spine as he bathed her nipples with his tongue, one after the other. She watched the flexing of his cheeks as he drew each of the rigid tips in turn into his mouth, gratifying his need for her. The breath hissed between his teeth, scorching her sensitive skin, when she reached down and took him, hard and hot, in her hand.

Luke couldn't believe the wonder of her. The resilient softness and responsive buds of her breasts, the flat plane of her stomach, the silk and satin of her thighs. Her lightest touch took him to heaven. Her every kiss was paradise. It seemed to him that he had waited a dozen lifetimes for her. As he raised his hips above hers and fused his body, his entire being with hers, he vowed to love her for a dozen more.

He lowered his brow to her shoulder and hoarsely sighed her name as he made her his. She felt warm and wet and so utterly exquisite he had to strain to hold himself back. Slow, sweet strokes gradually became harder, faster, more imperative.

Thrusting her hips up as he filled her with his hard warmth, Roxie gloried in the joy of being a woman. Of being *his* woman. She cried his name again and again, a pledge to him that she was his, forever, in every way possible.

The bedsprings squealed, his breath rasped, her mind reeled. She clung to the sweat-dampened muscles of his back as they shifted with each pump of pleasure. Her tummy tightened when he changed tempos, bringing her to a fever pitch of arousal.

Lifting his head, Luke saw the change in her expression and knew that she had reached the precipice. He joined her there, the beauty of her passion taking him to new heights. Then his body tightened and hers trembled as, together, they went over the edge.

Gradually, they slowed to stillness. Even as he rolled them to their sides, however, they remained twined together. Sated in body, bound in soul, they faced each other, smiling almost foolishly as they basked in a glorious afterglow.

Luke stroked the silk of her hair, working up the courage to say to her what he'd never said to anyone in his life. At length he whispered, "I love you, Roxie."

Roxie melted inside, simply melted. "I love you, too, Luke." She nipped at that beautiful, masculine bottom lip. "I realized I loved you the day you gave me the honey, but I never knew how much until now."

He grinned wickedly. "How much is that?"

She pinched her fingers together. "Oh, about this much."

He playfully swatted her bare bottom, then made up for it by kissing her breathless.

With his kiss desire clutched at Luke's belly, renewing itself. He didn't think he could ever get enough of her.

"I'll take what I can get," he said when he finally broke away, "and I'll give back to you, Roxie. I'll give anything to please you. I've missed you so much. Last week was hell."

"I was pretty miserable myself," she admitted. "Even Mr. Stewart noticed. He said I had to quit moping around and concentrate on business."

His lips toyed with her ear, then moved lower. "My pride has always been my downfall, but you always knew how to pierce my armor. I think that's why I first started to love you. You knew how to melt my foolish pride. You believed in me more than I believed in myself. Like coming here tonight, trusting in me."

Roxie hoped and prayed that he would think her suddenly jumping pulse stemmed from him kissing her neck. She must never, never let him know she'd doubted him, not even for a second. And truly, deep down in her heart, she hadn't doubted him at all. Her heart had led her straight to him.

Her mouth softened in a loving smile. "I always believed in you, right from the first. I was defending you even before you came to the warehouse for a job."

Luke's eyes probed into hers. "I thought then that you just felt sorry for me, and I resented it. At the time I thought I resented it because I didn't want to be anyone's charity case."

"But?" she prompted, sensing there was more.

"But the real reason was that I wanted your love, not your pity."

"Even then?" She tipped her head up. "You wanted my love

213

even back then?"

"Well," he drawled, that rakish smile returning in full force, "I certainly wanted your body."

Teasingly she tweaked a clump of his hair.

"Ouch!"

"You got it," she breathed, letting her fingers soothe his scalp. "You got it all."

He wanted to ask for how long, but he didn't want to press her. He didn't want her to shy away from him because he was too demanding. So he kissed her forehead and decided to change the subject.

"I found out who owns my grandfather's place."

Something about the way he said it made her heart race a little. "Who?"

"Your father."

Her jaw dropped. "My—"

"Your father's bank, to be more exact."

She couldn't believe it. "How did that happen?"

He leaned back a bit but kept his arms around her. "It's a long story."

"I'm not in a hurry."

He nudged her, and she felt him virile and warm against her belly. "I am, so I'll make this short."

"I'm all ears," she said in a throaty voice.

His hand swept down the supple curve from her breast to her hip to her thigh, and back up again. "I beg to differ."

Laughing, she settled in to listen.

"First, a little background," he said. "Granddad had a lot of admirable qualities, and, even though I wasn't good about showing it, I respected him for them. He was a man of the land, always working, always trying to scrape together enough money to keep his bills and his taxes paid. And he was honest—he wouldn't take the pennies off a dead man's eyes if he needed them to stave off starvation. But he was distant, beyond embrace."

He fell silent for a few seconds, as if what he had to say next would be difficult to put into words. Then he let out a resigned sigh and went on. "I think he always saw me as pretty much of a troublemaker. Which I was. And he always treated me like he was disappointed in me. Which he had every right to be."

She reached up and touched his lips, not to stop him from speaking but just to let him know that she had a totally different view of him.

"He wrote me the occasional letter while I was in prison. None of them more than a page long, usually half that." He smiled a little under serious eyes. "Once he sent one that said, 'No news.' That was it. 'No news.' " Luke's smile faded. "He never signed with 'love' or 'Granddad,' just his name, first and last. But as few and far between as they were, those letters were my lifeline to the outside, a reminder that someone hadn't forgotten I was on the inside."

He said it so matter-of-factly that it pierced her clean through. She debated telling him that she wouldn't have forgotten him either, but she didn't want to interrupt his train of thought.

After a short silence, he linked their fingers together and continued. "Anyway, I dreamed about him one night last week. I saw him plain as day striding out to check his beehives, climbing a wooden ladder to pick fruit off his trees, standing over his work bench in the honey house, reading his Bible at night by the light of an oil lamp. And then I remembered seeing him going to the bank with his hat in hand. *For what?* I wondered. Then I realized. He was going to try and borrow money on his land, his home so he could hire a lawyer to defend his good-for-nothing grandson."

Luke drew a ragged breath. "And that's when I knew."

Roxie sniffed back her tears. "He loved you."

Letting go of her hand, he sank his fingers into her still-damp hair and spread it out in a honey-gold fan on the bedspread behind her. "I knew, too, who probably owned the place. But I called the tax collector's office the next morning just to be sure, and they confirmed the bank was the owner of record."

"Dad has never said word one about it," she murmured.

"Remember the day you asked me why I came back to Blue Ridge?"

"Of course."

"I gave you a lot of reasons, but I didn't tell you the main one."

But she could guess. "You wanted to take care of his bees and his trees."

"It was too late to show him that somehow, somewhere along the line I could cut the mustard," he confirmed. "So I decided the best way to prove it, to honor both his memory and the man he was, was to try to bring back the place he loved."

Roxie was almost afraid to ask. "Does that mean you're staying here?"

"I want to, but I don't know if I can get the money together to buy the place back from the bank."

"It sounds like you need a partner." She waited a heart-stopping beat and then blurted, "Or a wife."

Luke could see in her eyes that she meant it, and wasn't that the miracle of all miracles? "Are you proposing to me, Roxie Mitchell?"

She laughed at her own audacity. "I certainly am, Luke Bauer."

He laughed, too. Then he sobered and leaned down to claim her mouth in a soul-searing kiss. She reached up and wrapped her arms around his neck, holding him as close to her heart as she could. Already, he was hard, and the blood was pumping hotly through her veins. Their kiss would have resulted in another round of lovemaking if someone hadn't pounded on his door.

They both shot up, gaping first at the door then at each other.

"Oh, my God," Luke said, and he scrambled off the bed to toss her a satin slip, a brasserie and underpants.

"What are you doing?" Roxie asked as this shower of lingerie splayed over her.

Another fervent knock reverberated through the small room.

"Get dressed." He yanked on his blue jeans and buttoned them as fast as he could. His head went to the left then the right. He scooped up her blouse and yelled, "I'm coming," then tossed the blouse to her.

She folded her hands in her lap and watched him.

"My God, aren't you dressed yet?" He looked around wildly. "The closet isn't very big, but if you're quiet—"

"Luke, I don't care," she said.

The hammering at the door became insistent.

He threw open the door to the closet and began pushing her clothes into it. "Come on, hurry up, if you're seen here, everyone will know—"

"I don't care if I'm seen," she said with emphasis.

He stopped shoving clothes into the closet and stared at her. She had never looked more like her mother, with the possible exception of a lack of clothing.

"You don't care?"

"Not if you plan to make an honest woman of me."

To the repeated banging on his door, Luke addressed a mild curse and an order to wait a minute. To the naked woman with the tender half smile sitting on his bed, he issued a rattled demand to know what she was talking about.

"I just proposed to you," she reminded him with a self-satisfied smile, "and you've yet to answer me."

The renewed pounding on the door had him flinging up his hands in surrender. "I accept. Now for God's sake, put something on. As lovely as I think your birthday suit is, I don't think anyone we know could stand the shock of seeing you in it."

"Thanks a lot," she said, laughing lightly as she slid out of the bed. She grabbed his work shirt, put it on to cover her nakedness and went to stand behind him as she buttoned it up to the neck.

Her slight shadow warmed his back. Luke set his hand on the knob and hoped with all his heart it wasn't a policeman who had come in connection with the problem at the warehouse. Once Roxie realized all the hassles that were a part of his life, she might take back her offer of marriage. And though he felt obligated to point out all the problems and the reasons against it, the one thing he wanted most in this life was to marry her. With suspicion and dread, he at last pulled open the door.

"It's about time!" Layton Stewart huffed, his Fedora dripping rainwater off the brim and onto the bare floor. "We were beginning to think you'd stashed a—" He stopped in his tracks just a foot over the threshold, and his brows rose as he took in the sight of his half-dressed employees standing together.

"Hi, Mr. Stewart." Roxie waved a floppy sleeve at him from behind Luke's back. "Luke and I are getting married."

"Oh . . . well . . . congratulations," he sputtered.

Luke looked at her over his shoulder. "Roxie, we only—"

"Hi, Gary," she said, ignoring Luke's attempt to speak. "Did you hear the news?"

"Yes, yes, I did." Like the innate gentleman he was, Gary had taken off his cap. Holding it in both hands in front of him, he averted his eyes from Roxie and looked more toward the peeling patch in the wall beside her. "May I add my congratulations to Mr. Stewart's?"

"You may," she said graciously and stepped out from behind Luke to accept his good wishes.

Neither the warehouse owner nor the warehouse manager could have been more shocked by her attire, or lack thereof, than Luke was by her actions. He hadn't expected her to tell anyone, much less to announce it so happily, so proudly. And he certainly hadn't expected her stand there half-dressed in front of the two men.

With difficulty he gathered himself together and said, "Hello, Mr. Stewart. Gary."

Layton Stewart looked like he'd been knocked flatter than a barn in a tornado. He ran his gaze over the bare-legged and bare-footed Roxie. "Well, I guess Mondays aren't so bad after all."

"I guess not," she agreed.

"And I don't suppose there's any need to ask if you're happy, since you're bright as a light with it."

"Glowing from head to toe," she chirped.

Now Layton Stewart turned his attention to Luke and said in a fatherly fashion, "You'd better be good to her, young man, or you'll answer to me."

Luke tensed at his warning until he saw how Roxie's face was shining. Then he softened. For her sake he would have to learn to accept these commonplace comments without thinking they held a challenge for him.

"I will, sir," he said. "You can count on it."

Gary waited stoically for the laughter to die away before clearing his throat. "Perhaps we should get on with the business at hand, Mr. Stewart, and then leave the two young ones alone."

"You're right as you almost always are, Gary." The warehouse owner turned back to Luke. "We came to tell you that today's problem has been cleared up. There never was any missing money."

"So what happened to it?" Roxie asked on behalf of both herself and Luke.

"Remember that Friday a few weeks ago when I left early so I could take Mrs. Stewart to St. Joseph to stay with our daughter and newborn grandson when they left the hospital?"

"Yes."

"Well, the day the deposit in question was made, last Friday, was also the day I went back to St. Joseph to pick up Mrs. Stewart and bring her home. It was a quick trip, up there one day and back here the next. I knew I wouldn't need much in the way of money, so I raided the cash we'd received that day."

Roxie's mouth fell open but she didn't interrupt him.

"At the time," he continued, "I made a note of the debit. But somewhere in my rush to get on my way, the note got lost. And in all the confusion this morning, I didn't have a clear enough head to think of it."

"You're sure?" Roxie said quietly.

"I'm wearing the same suit I wore to St. Joseph that day, and I found the note myself in the jacket pocket when I started for home this evening." He smiled with chagrin. "I called Gary, and we came right over here."

Gary put out his hand. "I want you to know, Luke, that even if Mr. Stewart hadn't found his note, I wanted you to stay on in the warehouse. You work hard and you do good work."

Luke took his hand. For the first time in his life he felt like an equal. He glanced at Roxie. With Roxie at his side, no matter where he wound up working he would be equal to any man on earth.

Layton Stewart saw the look that passed between the two and smiled. "When's the wedding?"

"Uh, we haven't set a date yet," Roxie replied. "But we'll let you know as soon as we do."

"Well, it's time we left you two alone." He patted her on the cheek, shook hands with Luke, and left with Gary.

Luke closed the door after them and got right to the point. "You can't really want to marry me, Roxie."

"Of course I can. I do."

"You want to live like this?" He glanced around at his shabby room.

"No, but then we aren't going to live like this. We'll fix up your grandfather's house and move in there after we're married. My parents have several nice old pieces in the attic that will look wonderful once they're refinished and—"

"And you're out of your mind." He put his hand flat over her mouth. "Now, just listen a minute and then think through what I'm about to say. Agreed?"

She nodded.

He removed his hand.

"But, Luke—" she began.

He put his hand back over her mouth and said bleakly, "You have to understand, Roxie, that every time there's money missing and I'm in the vicinity, I'll be under suspicion. As my wife, you'd be part of that. You'd be part of my past."

She pulled his hand away from her mouth but held onto it for dear life. "It's not where you've been that matters. It's where you're going."

"I know that, but there are people who look only at the trail behind you." Giving her fingers a gentle squeeze, he stared at her meaningfully. "Those are the people who will hurt you, Roxie, in a thousand little ways. And I don't want you hurt. Not at all, not ever."

"It would hurt me not to marry you," she said in all sincerity.

"I love you very much, but I'm not good enough for you."

"Of course you are."

He shoved his hair off his forehead with aggravated fingers. "I want to marry you more than anything I've ever wanted in my life, but—"

"And you're going to marry me. I love you, and I want to share the rest of my life with you. So when, do you think?"

He cradled her cheeks in his palms and gazed at her with such open love that her heart skipped erratically. "I'll marry you tonight if you really want me."

She solemnly studied his face, his ruggedly handsome face. His eyes were darkly silver, flashing and alive. His very masculine mouth was curved in a tenderly sweet smile. His dark hair fell boyishly over his brow. He looked younger and happier than she'd ever seen him.

Reaching out, she gently brushed his hair back. "I think that I've always known you were different. Even way back in school. Anytime the talk was about you, I sat up and listened. Anytime you were around, I stood and stared. Maybe I've always loved you, even all those years ago."

"Don't," he said. He trapped her hand within his and kissed it, front and back. "I don't want to think that you might have loved me then, that I might have escaped all the years of loneliness. I don't want to think of the might-have-beens. I only want to think about the will-bes in store for us."

"And the nows," she added, giving him a kiss.

"And the nows," he agreed, giving her his heart.

# ABOUT THE AUTHOR

**Fran Baker** has written eleven novels, with a twelfth in progress, as well as a couple hundred articles, humorous essays, op-ed pieces, book reviews, and author interviews. Her books have appeared on several bestseller lists and have been translated into more than twenty languages. Fran has conducted a number of writing workshops in the U.S. and in Canada, and she has spoken about writing for publication to local, national, and international audiences. She is a member of Novelists, Inc., the Authors Guild and the Society of Midland Authors; she blogs at DaughteroftheGreatDepression.blogspot.com and at RomancingTheYarn.blogspot.com with other authors who knit, and she is a contributing author at AWritersWork.com. Readers are invited to visit her Web site at www.FranBaker.com.